PALESTINE'S CHILDREN

RETURNING TO HAIFA & Other Stories

PALESTINE'S CHILDREN

RETURNING TO HAIFA & Other Stories

Ghassan Kanafani

translated by Barbara Harlow & Karen E. Riley,
with an Introduction and a Biographical Essay on Ghassan Kanafani

LYNNE
RIENNER
PUBLISHERS

BOULDER
LONDON

Published in the United States of America in 2000 by
Lynne Rienner Publishers, Inc.
1800 30th Street, Boulder, Colorado 80301
www.rienner.com

and in the United Kingdom by
Lynne Rienner Publishers, Inc.
Gray's Inn House, 127 Clerkenwell Road, London EC1 5DB

Library of Congress Cataloging-in-Publication Data
Kanafani, Ghassan.
  [Short stories. English. Selections]
  Palestine's children : Returning to Haifa and other stories / Ghassan
Kanafani; translated by Barbara Harlow and Karen E. Riley; with an introduction to
the work and a biographical essay on Ghassan Kanafani.
     p.   cm.
  Includes bibliographical references.
  ISBN 978-0-89410-865-5 (hc : alk. paper)
  ISBN 978-0-89410-890-7 (pb : alk. paper)
  1. Palestinian Arabs—Fiction. 2. Exiles—Palestine—Fiction. 3. Kanafâni,
Ghassân. I. Harlow, Barbara. II. Riley, Karen E. III. Title.
  PJ7842.A5   A24   2000
  892.7'36—dc21   00-024783

British Cataloguing in Publication Data
A Cataloguing in Publication record for this book
is available from the British Library.

Printed and bound in the United States of America

The paper used in this publication meets the requirements
of the American National Standard for Permanence of
Paper for Printed Library Materials Z39.48-1992.

20 19 18 17 16 15 14 13 12

Contents

Ghassan Kanafani: A Biographical Essay

KAREN E. RILEY

> My feelings are very strange. They are the feelings of a man
> who was on his way somewhere in search of suitable work
> when he died suddenly—on the road.[1]

Ghassan Kanafani was not yet twenty-four, teaching in a
Kuwaiti government school, when he wrote these words in a letter to a friend. The image is a precursor of his first major literary work, the novella *Men in the Sun,* written two years later. It
is also sadly prophetic of Kanafani's actual fate, for at the age of
thirty-six he did indeed die "suddenly," killed when his booby-
trapped car exploded in Beirut.

During Kanafani's brief life he was always "on his way
somewhere," always searching for the appropriate tool as well as
the most effective setting in which to use it. From his birth the
circumstances of his life were inextricably enmeshed with the
Palestinian cause. His "work" was survival, both his own and
that of his people, the Palestinians.

Ghassan Kanafani was born in Acre on the northern
Mediterranean coast of Palestine on April 9, 1936. That same
month, the Arab Higher Committee was established in response
to rapidly increasing Jewish immigration, and a general Arab

1

strike throughout Palestine was called by the committee to protest British mandatory government policies with respect to immigration. The strike paralyzed activity for six months.

Ghassan's father was a lawyer, and the family belonged to the upper middle class. He had an older sister and brother and three younger siblings. As was common at the time among the middle and upper classes, young Ghassan attended a school run by French missionaries in Palestine and was thus educated primarily in French rather than in the language of his own country. In his own words, he "did not have a command of the Arabic language like an Arab,"[2] and he would later make a conscious and serious effort to enrich his Arabic and rid it of foreign expressions.

In 1948, on his twelfth birthday, one of the most egregious events of the Zionist struggle for Palestine took place: the brutal massacre of the residents of an Arab village called Deir Yassin. Anni Kanafani, his widow, writes that Ghassan never celebrated his birthday after that year.[3] Within a month the city of Acre itself fell to Zionist forces, and his family escaped, first to a small village in southern Lebanon, then to the mountains outside Damascus, and finally to a ghetto in Damascus. There, the family's position changed dramatically.

In sudden exile and living in extreme poverty, the Kanafanis believed at first, like all the other Palestinians, that it would only be a matter of weeks, months, or a year at most before the situation would be reversed and they could go home. As a child Ghassan heard other Palestinian children playing in the camps and speaking with compassion of Syrian or Lebanese children, saying, "Poor things, they don't have Palestine to return to."[4]

Reality proved otherwise—it proved to be permanent exile. Ghassan took a keen interest in everything around him in the camps and noted the difference between his actual surroundings and his yearned-for past, and he began to draw and paint as a means of forging a link between that past and his miserable present.

When he was fourteen or fifteen years old, Ghassan broke his leg. He and two school friends had played hooky and gone into the mountains above Damascus, where Ghassan fell while trying to jump between boulders. Not wanting to admit his truancy to his father, he invented a clever story about a minor accident in town, and as a result, the leg was at first not treated properly. His convalescence stretched some six months, and he spent that time studying Arabic literature intensely in an effort to improve his usage and literary command of his native language.

At the age of sixteen he took a job teaching at a United Nations relief (UNRWA) school in a refugee camp, to help support his family as well as to continue his own education. His experiences even then were propelling him toward political involvement, and he would later state that he "turned toward politics at an early stage in life because we were living in a refugee camp."[5]

Two incidents while he was teaching are indicative of this propensity and illustrate the basis for his commitment to the Palestinian cause—a commitment that would develop through his life experiences and, in his literature, would symbolize and encompass the cause of all oppressed peoples seeking freedom. For one thing, he noticed that many of his young students were falling asleep during class, which angered him at first. But he then discovered that the children were working late into the night, selling sweets at the cinema or on the streets, to help support their families:

> I realized that the children's drowsiness did not stem from scorn for me or dislike of their studies, nor did it have anything to do with my capacity as a teacher. It was simply the reflection of a political problem.[6]

On another occasion Kanafani was giving a lesson in accordance with the official curriculum, which called for the instructor to teach the children how to draw an apple and a banana. While drawing these items on the blackboard, it suddenly occurred to him that these children had never seen either an apple or a banana; such things had no real bearing on their lives. So he erased his drawings and asked them to draw pictures of the refugee camp instead. He later described this event as a "decisive turning point" in his life, saying: "I clearly remember that precise moment among all the things that have happened to me in my life."[7]

During this same period, Kanafani enrolled at Damascus University in the Department of Arabic Literature. He began to write short stories that expressed realistically the Palestinians' desperate situation. He attracted the attention of some university students who had founded a literary society called the League of Literature and Life, and they persuaded him to join the group. But they were idealists for whom writing was a romanticized activity detached from and elevated above everyday life. Among them was Fadl al-Naqib, who would remain a lifelong friend and write his memoirs of Kanafani. In describing the difference between Kanafani and the other members of the group, for whom writing was a luxurious activity and publishing a dream for the future, al-Naqib says that Ghassan "devoted himself to publishing tomorrow what he wrote today. If he couldn't publish it in one magazine, he would try another. He lived without dreams."[8]

While at the university, Kanafani became active in student politics; this led him to Dr. George Habash, the leader of the Arab Nationalists' Movement, and he began to work in the movement. In 1955 he joined his brother and sister in Kuwait, where there was a large exiled Palestinian community, and took a job teaching in a government school. At the same time he continued his study of Arabic literature, returning to Damascus each summer for examinations.[9] He was barely twenty when he went to Kuwait, and despite the fact that his brother and sister were with him, he was beset by feelings of isolation, strangeness, and exile.

*   *   *

While Kanafani was in Kuwait, a personal calamity befell him that was to have a profound influence on his future. He was diagnosed as having severe diabetes; often losing consciousness, he had to learn to self-administer daily insulin injections. Face-to-face with his mortality, he began referring to it constantly in his letters and diaries. From Kuwait he once wrote:

> When I was twelve, just as I began to perceive the meaning of life and nature around me, I was hurled down and exiled from my own country. And now, now, just as I have begun to perceive my path . . . along comes "Mr. Diabetes" who wants, in all simplicity and arrogance, to kill me.[10]

His preoccupation at this stage was also mirrored by his equally pessimistic perception of the Palestinian situation. A diary entry from early 1960 reads:

> The only thing we know is that tomorrow will be no better than today, and that we are waiting on the banks, yearning, for a boat that will not come. We are sentenced to be separated from everything—except from our own destruction.[11]

Later that same year George Habash founded a new political magazine in Beirut called *al-Hurriyya* [*Independence*], and he asked Ghassan to join the editorial staff. Dropping everything, the young man went to Beirut in the summer of 1960 and, as he participated more actively and directly in Palestinian affairs, he managed to turn his absorption with his illness into an insatiable drive to accomplish as much as possible, to express as much as possible, using every available means. In describing his efforts to come to grips with his illness, he wrote to a friend:

> I tried to write about my illness, but I couldn't find anything to write. Therefore the matter seems to me to be very simple. The strongest form an illness takes is when it causes death, and that only happens to a man once. So as long as I am not dead, I am going to behave as though I am not sick.[12]

This matter-of-factness is apparent in an anecdote related by Fadl al-Naqib: Whenever Ghassan realized he needed insulin, he would blithely prepare and administer an injection, all the while talking with his companions, as though he were injecting someone else.[13] His widow has noted his "fantastic sense of humor," allowing him to be "rather joking with death—maybe in a tragical/comical way."[14] On occasion, for example, he would work to the point of forgetting the insulin altogether and have to be taken to the hospital for emergency treatment. It is said that after one such bout, Ghassan requested a cigarette. When the doctor refused, he countered:

> Doctor, this isn't the first time this has happened to me. Other times, the doctor has only given me one needle. I let you give me two needles, so you must let me have a cigarette. Life is give and take.

The doctor relented.[15]

*   *   *

In 1961 Kanafani met Anni Hoover, a Danish teacher who had come to Beirut to study the Palestinian refugee situation; in two months they were married. Since he had no passport at the time, he was forced to go underground in early 1962, and during this period of hiding he wrote *Men in the Sun,* dedicating it to Anni. When it was published the following year, it burst into the world of Arabic literature, bringing Kanafani instant and wide recognition and acclaim. It is still considered by many to be his best work.

Men in the Sun is about three exiled Palestinians who make arrangements in Iraq with a fourth to be smuggled over the border into Kuwait, where profitable employment is reputed to be available. The three hide in the empty water tank of a truck. When the driver—an embittered Palestinian exile who was castrated by a shell explosion in 1948—is detained at the border, the three men inside the tank suffocate silently under the blazing sun, "for fear of drawing the attention of the outside world to their existence."[16] The driver's agonized questions, "Why didn't you knock on the sides of the tank? Why didn't you say anything? Why?" are echoed back by the desert at the novella's end, an echo that rang in the ears of the entire Palestinian community like a provocation.

That same year, Kanafani also became editor-in-chief of a new daily in Beirut, *al-Muharrir* [*The Liberator*], which included a weekly supplement called *Filastin* [*Palestine*], also edited by him. Both were widely respected and quoted throughout the Arab world. From this point on, Kanafani's work intensified. He was contributing to many daily and weekly publications at the same time, in addition to writing fiction. Because of the recognition *Men in the Sun* had brought, friends and critics tried to convince him to spend less time on journalism and concentrate on his literary writing. In a letter shortly after the publication of *Men in the Sun,* Kanafani wrote:

> Now the advice from my friends to pay less attention to journalism is growing stronger. In the end, as they put it, journalism will destroy my artistic ability to write stories. In truth, I don't understand this logic. It is the same logic I used to hear in school: leave politics and concentrate on your studies, and later in Kuwait, give up writing and take care of your health. Did I really have a choice between studies and politics, between writing and health, or now between journalism and stories? I want to say something. Sometimes I can say it in the official news of the morning, sometimes fashioned into an editorial, or into a small piece on the society page. Sometimes I can't say what I want to say in anything but a story. The choice they talk about is nonexistent. It reminds me of the Arabic teacher who at the beginning of each school year asks the children to write an essay on whether they prefer life in the village or life in the city — and the children live in a refugee camp![17]

He accepted the fact that all the aspects of his life were interconnected. Just as politics shaped events, so his work—both what he wrote and how he wrote—was structured by those events, and they were reflected in it.

* * *

In 1965, the first armed struggle to regain Palestine was launched, a year after the Palestine Liberation Organization (PLO) was founded. These developments reverberated in the Palestinian community, affecting not only Palestinian life but also its literature; the questions pending at the end of *Men in the Sun* now assumed the shape of political action. For the first time since 1948, the Palestinians were taking their struggle and their future into their own hands, neither relying on external Arab armies nor denying their history and identity by dying silently in exile. Kanafani's work now had a "relatively more optimistic outlook . . . as a result of the establishment of the Palestine Liberation Organization in 1964 and the launching of armed struggle the following year."[18]

Then came the disastrous war of 1967. On June 5, Kanafani sat listening to the news reports at *al-Muharrir*'s headquarters. When he noticed that all of the reports were identical, he became suspicious and contacted friends and army personnel, only to learn of the Arabs' defeat. At the end of the day he was left alone in the office, to write the editorial for the morning paper. He described this moment as being the first time in his life that he lost the ability to write. But even after this defeat, he remained resolute and optimistic, encouraging others even when he himself felt despair. As Anni Kanafani put it: "In critical moments he was unbelievably strong and tried to give some of that strength to others. Later on he would express his feelings in political and literary writings."[19] One of the literary works to come out of this particular "critical moment" was *Returning to Haifa*.

*   *   *

Shorty after the June 1967 war, Kanafani left *al-Muharrir* to join the prestigious daily *al-Anwar* [*The Lights*] as editor-in-chief of its weekly magazine. In 1969, he left that position to cofound a new political newspaper called *al-Hadaf* [*The Goal*], which became the organ of the Popular Front for the Liberation of Palestine (PFLP), the successor organization to George Habash's Arab Nationalists' Movement. The PFLP was Marxist-oriented, committed not only to regaining the homeland in Palestine, but also to the establishment of a new secular society based on social reform and social justice both in Palestine and throughout the Arab world.

In 1969 he published *Returning to Haifa* and *Umm Saad* [*Saad's Mother*], the latter a vivid portrayal of life in the refugee camps structured as a series of conversations between the narrator and a woman from the camp whose son has joined the Palestinian resistance. In both works, Kanafani places the future in the hands of the new generation of Palestinians, whose commitment and emotional ties to Palestine are stronger than the more concrete connections experienced by their parents.

In 1970, in the course of a long conversation with a friend, Kanafani was asked whether he was optimistic. He replied that he was indeed. In the past, he said, Palestinians would wait to read the news and then react to it with optimism or pessimism. But now, for the first time, Palestinians could be optimistic because they knew in advance what the news would say. Kanafani's friend then asked him if he knew the story of the reporter who had asked George Bernard Shaw, on his ninetieth birthday, how it felt to be ninety. Shaw replied that he felt very happy, considering the alternative. Kanafani laughed heartily and at length, then grew serious:

> Today isn't my birthday, but if you asked me how I feel I would not hesitate to say I feel happy, not because I consider the alternative, but because I know we are traveling on a path for which there is no alternative.[20]

During 1970–1972, political and armed activity intensified. The PLO carried out a number of attacks against Israel from Lebanon and Jordan. Internal political pressures led Jordan to expel the PLO in 1971. In 1972 Red Army gunmen attacked Lod Airport outside Tel Aviv and a telephone caller claimed responsibility on behalf of the PFLP.

On July 8, 1972, Ghassan Kanafani and his niece Lamees got into his car. Lamees was his sister's daughter, and Ghassan had adored her from the moment she was born. Every year on her birthday he sent her a hand-written book of stories or poetry illustrated with his own drawings. When Ghassan started the motor, the booby-trapped car exploded, killing them both. The act was generally considered to be a reprisal for the Lod Airport attack.[21]

Anni Kanafani was inside the house with their nine-year-old son, Fayez. Their daughter Laila, who was five, was sitting on the steps of the house eating some chocolate her father had just given her. The explosion blew out all the windows of the house. Anni ran down the stairs and saw the wreckage of the car:

> We found Lamees a few meters away, Ghassan wasn't there. I called his name—then I discovered his left leg. I stood paralyzed, while Fayez knocked his head against the wall and our daughter Laila cried again and again: "Baba, Baba . . ."[22]

Anni Kanafani led the massive funeral procession through the streets of Beirut, Fayez by her side. Ghassan's remains were wrapped in the Palestinian flag, and as his body was lowered into its final place, it is said that his young son raised his fingers in the sign of victory. Many of Kanafani's characters, including the protagonist of *Returning to Haifa,* saw victory in the sacrifice of their sons to the Palestinian cause. In the end, Kanafani's own son saw victory in the sacrifice of his father.

*　　*　　*

During the brief and tumultuous journey of his life, Ghassan Kanafani searched. Not for work, for he knew what his work was; instead, he persevered in looking for the best means to carry out that work. He turned his own struggle for survival against illness into a source of energy to fight for the survival of the Palestinian people. First a paint brush, then a pencil, then arms—Ghassan used every weapon available to defend himself and his people.[23] Even the insulin needle he wielded so expertly was a weapon in the battle, used to defend himself from death and purchase precious time to lengthen his journey, expand his search.

Fadl al-Naqib said of Ghassan Kanafani: "He wrote the Palestinian story, then he was written by it."[24] During a particular twenty-year period in Palestinian history, Kanafani's unconditional commitment to the survival of the Palestinian people and his tremendous journalistic and literary output made it possible for him not just to write stories, but to write *the* Palestinian story, made it possible for that story to continue to be written, and lived, today.

Notes

1. Ghassan Kanafani, "Diary 1959–1960" [*sic*] (excerpts from diary entries covering the period 1959–1962) [Arabic], *Carmel* (spring 1981): p. 242. (Hereafter referred to as "Diary.")

2. "An Interview Published for the First Time: With the Martyr Ghassan Kanafani" [Arabic], *Palestinian Affairs* 35 (July 1974): p. 136. (Hereafter referred to as "An Interview.")

3. Anni Kanafani, *Ghassan Kanafani* (Beirut: Palestine Research Center, 1973), unnumbered. (Hereafter referred to as "A. Kanafani.") Initially the death toll at Deir Yassin was reported to have been approximately 250, a figure widely held as accurate. Subsequent scholarship indicates that the number of dead actually may have been around 100 and that the Zionists may have perpetuated belief in the higher figure to further instill terror in the Arab population.

4. Fadl al-Naqib, "The World of Ghassan Kanafani" [Arabic], *Palestinian Affairs* 13 (September 1972), p. 193.

5. "An Interview," p. 137.

6. Ibid.

7. Ibid.

8. Fadl al-Naqib, *Thus Stories End, Thus They Begin* [Arabic] (Beirut: Muassassat al-Abhath al-Arabiyya, 1983), pp. 14–15.

9. Personal correspondence from Anni Kanafani to the translator, June 28, 1990. It is sometimes reported, incorrectly, that Ghassan Kanafani was expelled from Damascus University for his political activity.

10. al-Naqib, "The World of Ghassan Kanafani," p. 196.

11. "Diary," 241.

12. al-Naqib, "The World of Ghassan Kanafani," pp. 196–197.

13. Ibid.

14. Personal correspondence from A. Kanafani.

15. al-Naqib, *Thus Stories End*, p. 89.

16. Muhammad Siddiq, *Man is a Cause: Political Consciousness and the Fiction of Ghassan Kanafani* (Seattle: University of Washington Press, 1984), p. 87.

17. al-Naqib, "The World of Ghassan Kanafani," p. 200.

18. Siddiq, p. 89.

19. A. Kanafani.

20. al-Naqib, "The World of Ghassan Kanafani," p. 203.

21. On January 22, 1973, the *Jerusalem Post* reported that Israeli agents were responsible for Ghassan Kanafani's assassination. Raphael Rothstein, U.S. correspondent for *Haaretz,* reported the same in *World Magazine* in an article entitled, "Undercover Terror: The Other Mid-East War." (Both articles cited in A. Kanafani.) Zeev Schiff, historian of the Israeli military forces, states that the assassinations of Kanafani and others were in response to Palestinian acts, and adds: "Israel is careful not to take credit officially for these actions." Zeev Schiff, *A History of the Israeli Army 1870–1974,* tr. Raphael Rothstein (San Francisco: Straight Arrow Books, 1974), p. 237.

22. A. Kanafani.

23. al-Naqib, "The World of Ghassan Kanafani," p. 201.

24. al-Naqib, *Thus Stories End,* p. 7.

Introduction

KAREN E. RILEY & BARBARA HARLOW

F OR NEARLY A CENTURY, POLITICS, VIOLENCE, AND diplomacy have all failed to resolve the complex, mythified, and misunderstood clash that since 1948 has come to be known as the Arab-Israeli conflict. Certainly it is not for lack of study; books on the subject in English alone could fill a small-town library. Perhaps what has been missing—or ignored—throughout is the quotidian human reality underlying the vital history that continues to connect Palestinians everywhere to the land once called Palestine. Often, literature can provide the human dimension that the historian's work alone cannot. The literary works of the Palestinian writer Ghassan Kanafani resonate with precisely that human dimension.

*   *   *

Ghassan Kanafani's activities as a writer were diverse, ranging from journalism and political essays to historical studies, theater, and literary criticism. As a journalist and critic, he played an important role in introducing new authors and their works to Arab readers. It was Kanafani as well who, in his study on the "Literature of Resistance in Occupied Palestine," first employed

13

the term "resistance" (*muqawamah*) in speaking of Palestinian literature. His fiction, including short novels, stories, and children's literature—the stories and poems composed for his niece Lamees—represents a major contribution to modern Arabic literature. The stories, however, like Kanafani's other writings, address specifically the Palestinian situation. Kanafani describes the political, social, and human realities that characterize the lives of his people at a critical period in their history, when the traditional order and structure of their existence are being profoundly altered by events on both a regional and international scale. Kanafani's stories tell of mothers in the refugee camps who proudly send their sons to the *fidayeen* and who then visit them in the mountains with gifts of food from home, of fathers whose role of authority within the family is being threatened by the transformations in their social world, of children who learn early to fight for a place in that social order, of concern and love and fear and suspicion among neighbors who feel threatened by strangers in their land.

The stories and novella translated in this volume are all set between 1936 and 1967. Many have as their temporal locus the year 1948. The dates mark significant moments in the twentieth-century history of the Palestinians, for in 1936 there began in Palestine a widespread popular revolt and 1967 saw a serious check, in the form of the June War, to Palestinian national aspirations. In 1948, the state of Israel was founded, an event accompanied by the massive displacement of Palestinians from their homeland and the beginning of the years and then decades of exile. Each of the stories here involves in some way a child, a child who, though victimized by the structures of authority that dominate the social and political world he lives in, nonetheless, by assuming new roles, participates personally in the struggle toward a new and different kind of future.

Kanafani's stories present a Palestinian perspective on a conflict that has anguished the Middle East and the Arab world for most of the twentieth century. It is a perspective that is vital to understand and to acknowledge, the product of the experience of decades of dispossession and struggle that, although not unique to the Palestinians, finds in them both a real and a symbolic expression. It is this experience that must be taken into account in considering the violence and brutal intensity of some of the stories in this volume, a violence that is at the same time rendered problematic in the internal conflicts of the characters themselves and in their literary and historical setting.

The stories are told from the point of view of the children of Palestine by a writer who was long involved with their education and development. Kanafani, who attended the UNRWA schools for Palestinian refugees in Damascus after he left Palestine with his family in 1948, later became a teacher in those same schools. The years he spent as a student and teacher were to have a significant effect on his subsequent development as a writer.

The tension between the political and historical events and their literary transformation distinguishes the writings of Ghassan Kanafani. Through narrative, historical necessities lose their implacableness as faits accomplis and become rich with possibility. According to Fawaz Turki, another Palestinian writer, "If the Palestinian revolution is armed with a philosophy at all, it is armed with the anti-determinist vision of the open-endedness of the future."[1] It is the open-endedness of the future that Kanafani creates and that becomes visible in his literary exposition of the events of Palestinian history.

Both "The Child Goes to the Camp" (1967) and "A Present for the Holiday" (1968) are set in the Palestinian refugee camps. These camps were first created in 1950 in order to provide temporary shelter and sustenance for those people who were obliged to flee their homes in Palestine in 1948. They were further populated by another generation of refugees in 1967, following the June War, when the areas now known as the West Bank and the Gaza Strip were occupied by Israel. Life in the camps thus acquired a significance over time and a history that has become crucial to the Palestinian experience. The children who came in 1948 gave birth to children of their own, the *awlad al-mukhayyamat* or "children of the camps." This historical significance of the camp life is unavailable, however, to the child-narrator of "The Child Goes to the Camp." For him, it was a relentless present, a "time of hostilities," in which finding five pounds in the street while he and his cousin Isam were collecting leftover produce from the market for the family's meal was sufficient to mark a turning point in his day-to-day existence. "It was war-time," the story begins, only to qualify its terms. "Not war really, but hostilities, to be precise . . . a continued struggle with the enemy. In war, the winds of peace gather the combatants to repose, truce, tranquility, the holiday of retreat. But this is not so with hostilities which are always never more than a gunshot away, where you are always walking miraculously between the shots. That's what it was, just as I was telling you, a time of hostilities." The conflicts exist within the society and inside the traditional order. "The whole thing is that there were eighteen people from different generations living in one house, which would have been more than enough at any time. . . . We fought for our food and then fought each other over how it would be distributed amongst us. Then we fought again." Historical time has collapsed into hostile disorder, and past, present, and future generations vie with each other for immediate control over the administration of five pounds.

In "A Present for the Holiday," even commemorative time has lost its ritual significance and symbolic value. The narrator has been awakened by a telephone call from a friend who has plans for a project to distribute holiday presents to the children newly arrived in the refugee camps following the 1967 war. "I was half asleep. The camps. Those stains on the forehead of our weary morning, lacerations brandished like flags of defeat, billowing by chance above the plains of mud and dust and compassion." The story of the telephone call, interrupted by the narrator's recollections of his own childhood in the camps, is punctuated by the recurrent refrain: "But all that is beside the point." Its repetition suspends the movement from past to future in the meaninglessness of the present.

"Guns in the Camp" (1969), still another story that has as its setting the Palestinian refugee camps, describes a transformation within the life of the camps, a transformation motivated by the emergence of a budding resistance movement. The story is one of a series of episodes that tell the history of Umm Saad, a Palestinian mother who, as her husband Abu Saad proudly says of her, "has borne sons who have grown up to become *fidayeen*. She provides the children for Palestine." The resistance movement becomes symbolic of a re-entry that would confer meaning on the past and create possibilities for the future. "'The grapevine is blooming, cousin! The grapevine is blooming!' I stepped towards the door where Umm Saad was bent over the dirt, where there grew—since a time which at that moment seemed to be infinitely remote—the strong firm stems which she had brought to me one morning. A green head sprouting through the dirt with a vigour that had a voice of its own." Here the rootedness of the plant in the soil stands as a symbolic counterweight to the historical forces of displacement and dispersion. The alienation of dispossession is made to acquire through the literary and poetic images a creative power of its own.

Through the narrative, however, perhaps even more importantly than through the imagery, Kanafani's stories contend with chronology and its closures. In telling these stories, stories of the Palestinian people and their children, Kanafani is retelling their history and re-establishing its chronology. The epic flashback no less than the stream-of-consciousness serves to confute the sense of time and temporality. Historical dates become commemorative, "so that people would say," as in an early story by Kanafani, "'it happened a month after the day of the massacre'."[2] Works of literature, stories and novels, are brought then to participate in the historiographic process. The political immediacy and historicity of these stories are, however, as much a part of a literary project as it is the case that literature will be used in the service of a given historical vision. Of his own relationship to literature and politics, Kanafani has said, "My political position springs from my being a novelist. In so far as I am concerned, politics and the novel are an indivisible case and I can categorically state that I became politically committed because I am a novelist, not the opposite. I started writing the story of my Palestinian life before I found a clear political position or joined any organization."[3]

Kanafani's stories and literary histories are located within a specific historical context. It is a context, however, whose very determinism the stories call into question through their narrative examination of interpretation and the parameters of storytelling. The questioning is undergone as well by the characters themselves in each of the stories. Four of these stories recount the coming of age of Mansur, a child from the Galilee village of Majd al-Kurum, who participates in a series of armed conflicts surrounding the establishment in 1948 of the state of Israel. Mansur's stories (1965) are: "The Child Borrows His Uncle's Gun and Goes East to Safad," "Doctor Qassim Talks to Eva About Mansur Who Has Arrived in Safad," "Abu al-Hassan Ambushes an English Car," and "The Child, His Father, and the Gun Go to the Citadel at Jaddin." Mansur must find someone from whom he can borrow a gun in order to join the battle being waged by the villagers at Safad. Guns, however, are the possessions of adults, his father, his uncle, the older men of the villages, and Mansur is subject to their authority. If his father is not interested in his ideals of resistance and patriotism, Mansur's uncle, Abu al-Hassan, tells him that he is too young, that he is just a child. And Hajj Abbas wants to negotiate a financial arrangement. Doctor Qassim, Mansur's older brother, meanwhile is having breakfast with Eva, a Jewish girl in Haifa.

In telling the story of the child Mansur's role in the 1948 struggle, Kanafani narrates the larger political and social conflicts created within the Palestinian community from outside. According to Ann Lesch, a political historian of Palestine under the British Mandate, "the generational differences within the Arab political leadership played an important political role. The older politicians tended to be more conciliatory, more willing to work within legal channels than the young men, [but] the impact of the generational division was reduced by the Arabs' deferential culture. Respect for one's father and for an elder statesman who consulted the other leaders and expressed the general consensus remained powerful forces, drawing together the differing drives of young and old in a politically effective manner."[4] At the same time, then, that the social order of Palestinian life is being attacked by foreign forces, the traditional structures of authority serve to sustain vital elements of the sense of community and solidarity. The authoritative structures, however, are being radically modified by the forces of circumstance and the political coming of age of the child. When Mansur at last reaches the citadel at Jaddin, his second expedition following upon the skirmish at Safad, he finds his father present there in the circle of armed men. In the moment of retreat, however, Abu Qassim is left behind. It is Mansur who returns for him, only to find him fatally wounded. "Mansur stood in the wet emptiness watching his father slowly dying, impotent and unmoving except for the deep throbbing which shook him. His veins were like taut wires bulging from his hands and extending around the torso of the gun. Finally they all began to blur together: the tree, the man and the gun, from behind the darkness of the angry rain, and through his tears. But to Mansur, they were not together. There was only the quiet corpse."

Mansur, on his way to participate in the events of Palestine's history, has traversed the Galilean countryside, visiting its villages, skirting its fields, and making his way across the junctions of its thoroughfares. Like other of Kanafani's stories, including "Paper from Ramleh" (1956) and "He Was a Child That Day" (1969), the fictional narratives provide not only a historical account of Palestine, but a topographical record as well. Much of the area and its villages no longer exist as they once did; they have been not only obliterated by the passage of time, but destroyed, rebuilt, and renamed by political events. What James Joyce did for Dublin or William Faulkner for the U.S. South, Kanafani in his stories has provided for Palestine. The intimate connection between history and the land is essential to Palestinian political and cultural ideology, its poetry, its processes, and its praxis. Despite the transformations and reinterpretations to which it has been subjected, the stories' record is there.

Returning to Haifa has two historical settings, roughly twenty years apart: 1948 and 1967. The primary action takes place a few weeks after the end of the June 1967 war in which Israel captured the West Bank, Sinai, Gaza, and the Golan. For the first time since 1948, the borders between pre-1967 Israel and the West Bank and Gaza are opened by the Israelis for passage by Palestinians. As the novella's protagonists, Said S. and his wife Safiyya, make their way from their West Bank home in Ramallah back to Haifa, their former home, their thoughts are interwoven with memories of the events of April 21, 1948, when they, along with thousands of Haifa's Palestinian residents, left the city in a panicked exodus as it changed overnight from British to Jewish control. The dramatic flight of Palestinians during the battle for Haifa forms the central image of *Returning to Haifa*'s opening chapter and also the axis around which the protagonists' lives develop and much of the novella's later dialogue revolves.

In February 1947, Great Britain, the mandatory power governing Palestine since the aftermath of World War I, announced that the mandate had become unworkable due to the increasingly violent and uncontrollable conflict between the native Palestinians and Zionists intent on their goal of establishing a Jewish homeland in Palestine. Britain's decision to relinquish Palestine upon expiration of the mandate pushed the matter into the hands of the United Nations, which recommended partition into Arab and Jewish states.

From that point on, fierce struggles ensued for control as the British began to evacuate city after city and the Jewish forces sought to secure not only the territory allotted for a Jewish state but also territory allotted for an Arab state by the United Nations partition plan. By May 14, 1948, the day on which Israel declared its statehood, at least 200,000 Palestinians had fled Palestine; by the end of the war that ensued, some 700,000 had become refugees. Many settled in West Bank towns, and approximately 150,000 Palestinians remained within the borders of what became the state of Israel. In the aftermath of the war, Jordan annexed the West Bank, and the Palestinians living there came under Jordanian rule. The situation remained thus for nearly twenty years until, in June 1967, the borders between the original state of Israel and the territories captured in the Six Day War were opened to Palestinians for passage. Refugees who had settled in the West Bank or Gaza could now return to see their old homes. Children too young to remember 1948, and children born in exile, were now able to see for the

first time the homes they knew of only from their parents'
reminiscences.

The opening of the border between Israel and the newly
occupied territories in 1967 allowed the exiled Palestinians to
confront physically their past lives, and at the same time forced
a psychological confrontation with the reasons for that exile. It
is not surprising, therefore, that Ghassan Kanafani should
explore this collision[5] within the framework of a novella, since
all of his fiction is intimately tied to the emotional heart of the
Palestinian community, not just reflecting it but actually consti-
tuting a vital part of that community's psychological evolution.

In *Returning to Haifa*, that psychological evolution is
reflected by Kanafani's juxtaposition of the events of 1948 and
1967. Radwa Ashur points out that Said's and Safiyya's journey
back to Haifa is representative of the Palestinian people as a
whole at that stage facing up to its responsibility for losing, or
"abandoning," Palestine and the fruitlessness of having spent
twenty years doing little more than crying over the loss.[6]
Kanafani recreates that sense of loss and fruitlessness by paralleling the political events of 1967 with the "abandonment" of
the infant Khaldun in 1948. By layering the two settings, he
captures the fundamental influence that the loss continued to
exert on the Palestinians' existence, remaining with them "in
every bite of food" they took throughout the intervening twenty
years. This duality of psychological and political exile is also
projected by Kanafani's narrative style. Referring to *Men in the
Sun*, Edward Said writes:

> Kanafani's very sentences express instability and fluctua-
> tion—the present tense is subject to echoes from the past,
> verbs of sight give way to verbs of sound or smell, and one
> sense interweaves with another—in an effort to defend
> against the harsh present and to protect some particularly
> cherished fragment of the past.[7]

His commentary is particularly applicable to *Returning to
Haifa*, since the novella's very structure is based on reliving in
the present a past event at the site where it first took place.
Transitions from past to present and vice-versa occur seemingly

arbitrarily, in the same way that memory and reality intermingle, giving the novella a sense of temporal ambiguity.

The present itself is experienced as if it were already a memory, already lost, such as when Safiyya, in the midst of her desperate flight through Haifa, realizes that she has left her infant son behind. She feels she will never again be able to face her husband, and is frightened that she is "about to lose them both—Said and Khaldun." She becomes aware that the memory of the present moment will have bitter repercussions on the future. It is a poignant portrayal of the sense of loss, brilliantly fashioned by Kanafani.

The imagery in *Returning to Haifa* is also marked by this relationship between time and space, between loss and memory, concretizing the pivotal role played by memory in the emotional and physical condition endured by the Palestinian exile as a result of the cataclysmic loss suffered in 1948. When, for example, Said first catches sight of his former house in Haifa, he sees it not as it is, but as he remembers it, and instantaneously he imagines that his wife, "young again with her hair in a long braid," will step out onto the balcony. Immediately upon the heels of this interplay of memory inside Said's mind, Kanafani inserts a statement describing something new and different about what Said is looking at, skillfully looping past, present, and future together: past, because of Said's memories; present because he is pulled back from recollection; and future, because the vivid detail heightens the expectation that something "new and different" may happen to Said. This congruence of imagery and temporal interaction simultaneously evokes the loss of Safiyya's youth as well as the loss of the home in which they once lived and, by extension, the loss of Palestine. At the same time, it foreshadows the change in Said, his ultimate recognition that man is indeed a cause and his discovery of "the true Palestine, the Palestine that's more than memories, more than peacock feathers, more than a son, more than scars written by bullets on the stairs."

Such images are implicit, in that they convey a multidimensional unit of time triggered by the sight of the house. Other images are explicit, such as when, near the novella's conclusion,

Said reflects that his memories of his child are nothing more than "a handful of snow" melted by the sun. Forced to confront the reality of the past—the old/new house, the old/new inhabitants, the old/new son—Said recognizes that the past has "melted" and been replaced by a new reality. He has made, in effect, a judgment, and with it, a new commitment.

There is, in addition, a certain dissonance in Kanafani's imagery that serves to highlight not only the violence of 1948, but also its brutal abruptness and the powerlessness felt by the Palestinians in the face of it. There is little sense of the normal passage of time, for example: events occur "suddenly" or characters "suddenly" become aware of something—such as the sound of the ocean—or of events or feelings that normally one would perceive gradually. There are images of violence and destruction: "walls collapse" in conveying the recall of a memory; people are "hurled down" or struck by an "electric shock" as a result of verbal exchanges that cause mental rather than physical confrontation. Frequently, these images are internalized, as when names "rain down inside" a protagonist's head.

All of these aspects of Kanafani's style make translation especially difficult because an exact rendering can result in unconventional or even awkward English. Yet it is critical to accentuate such ambiguities of tense or image in order to maintain the integrity of the original as an expression of the Palestinians' emotional, psychological, and political conflict and frustration.

Politics imposes itself on Kanafani's style in yet another, but more indirect manner. He wrote extensively—indeed, daily in later years—for newspapers and political and news magazines or journals. His commitment both to the Palestinian cause and to the craft of writing was so strong that he felt compelled to capture each moment of Palestinian experience by expressing himself in every genre available to him, despite advice from friends and critics that he put aside journalism and concentrate on literature. The year in which *Returning to Haifa* was published, 1969, was one of intense journalistic activity for him, as he founded and became editor-in-chief of *al-Hadaf*. In *Returning to Haifa* certain repetitive expressions appear frequently, paralleling journalistic Arabic, which tends to employ formulaic expressions that are recognizable as the accepted way of making certain statements. As such, notably in a late work like *Returning to Haifa,* these recurrences constitute an element of Kanafani's style that is directly related to the circumstances of his own life as well as his political position.

At the time Kanafani wrote *Returning to Haifa,* he was formulating a sense of the Palestinian struggle as one of social and political justice. In an interview he once stated:

> At first I wrote about Palestine as a cause in and of itself. . . .
> Then I came to see Palestine as a symbol of humanity. . . .
> When I portray the Palestinian misery, I am really presenting the Palestinian as a symbol of misery in all the world.[8]

As noted earlier, in 1969 he became the official spokesman of the Marxist PFLP, and his other fictional work of that year, *Umm Saad,* explores the issues of oppression and class struggle that lead to political action and social revolution.

In *Returning to Haifa,* he approaches these philosophical explorations differently. The two Jewish characters, Iphrat Koshen and his wife Miriam, far from being Zionist zealots, are portrayed instead as ordinary Jews fleeing Nazi Poland, misled by idealized Zionist literature into expecting something quite different from the reality they found upon reaching Palestine. Ashur credits Kanafani with the first attempt in Arabic literature to portray Jewish characters as sensitive human beings rather than as caricatures of the enemy.[9] When Miriam sees a dead Arab child being tossed into the garbage by a Jewish soldier, she identifies the child with her own young brother, killed before her eyes by the Nazis, and she wants to leave Palestine immediately. Of Miriam, Ashur notes:

> Ghassan Kanafani relates, by means of this character and her history, for the first time in Arabic literature, the agony of oppressed peoples in all places, the agony of Palestinians at the hands of the Zionists and the agony of the Jews at the hands of the Nazis.[10]

Miriam and Iphrat, however, do not leave Palestine, despite their initial moral misgivings. The justifications for their remaining, along with the reasons for the Palestinians' departure, are explored by Kanafani through the device of a conversation among the Arab and Jewish protagonists, set in what had once been Said's and Safiyya's house. According to critic F. Mansur, the dialogue between these characters represents

> the first time the Palestinian and the Jew meet each other, not on the battlefield but in a normal room, where each of them puts forth his point of view and discusses it with the other.[11]

The discussion is as thought-provoking to the reader today as it was to the Palestinian community at the time it was written.

Kanafani was a highly successful journalist, widely published and read. Yet, he continued to write stories. If his only aim had been the expression of political ideology and analysis, he would have had ample opportunity to do so without undertaking the additional task of creating an artistic framework for his ideas. To concentrate, therefore, exclusively on the symbolism or the political or ideological posture of *Returning to Haifa* is to lose sight of an important aspect of its value and impact. Like all of Kanafani's works, *Returning to Haifa* is realistic, filled with the physical details and vital turns of emotion of both everyday life and momentous historical events. According to Ashur, it is this "piercing grasp of reality" that distinguishes Kanafani's works from the greater part of Palestinian fiction which, up to that point, tended to rely on the sympathy it might arouse in the reader but which inevitably presented a false or flat picture that "ignored the full dimensions and complications" making up the reality of the situation.[12]

Kanafani himself on numerous occasions expressed the importance of realism: "In my novels I express reality, as I understand it, without analysis."[13] In an interview given shortly before his death and published posthumously, several of his comments shed light on the importance he gave to this aspect of his writing:

I think the greatest influence on my writing goes back to reality itself, what I witnessed, the experiences of my friends and
family and brothers and students, my life in the camps with
poverty and misery.

I didn't choose my characters for artistic literary reasons. All
of them came from the camp, not from outside of it.

When I review all the stories I have written about Palestine
up to now, it seems to me that every story is tied, directly or
indirectly, by a thin or strong thread, to my personal experiences in life.[14]

An earlier statement about his aims sums up the relationship
between realism and symbolism or ideology in his fictional
works: "I want my stories to be one hundred percent realistic
while at the same time presenting *something unseen.*"[15]

In *Returning to Haifa* it is the realistic details that lead to
the "something unseen." The portrayal of the mass exodus from
Haifa is gripping and vivid not only because it is grounded in
historical fact, but because Kanafani renders it with acute sensitivity. The minute details of Said's and Safiyya's house in Haifa,
and their "rediscovery" of those details, vibrate with feeling and
reveal their relationship to the house now and in their memories. The atmosphere is emotionally charged and builds up as
the novella unfolds with quiet intensity, preparing the reader
for the climactic dialogue that explodes into the "something
unseen": the human and emotional dimension underlying the
political dilemma of the Palestinian question for more than
forty years.

Mansur states that *Returning to Haifa* is Kanafani's "master-
piece . . . his most mature work," and goes on to postulate that
"after *Returning to Haifa,* there was no room to doubt that
when the definitive Palestinian novel was written, its author
would be Ghassan Kanafani."[16] These statements have validity
precisely because this work is more than a "historical political
document." The political dynamics have changed in the intervening years since it was written, but the social dynamics that
characterize the Palestinian conflict have not. Two generations

after 1948, people's lives continue to be disrupted at the most elemental levels as a result of what happened in 1948. The human dimension is what Ghassan Kanafani succeeds in expressing through the images, the narrative style, and the compelling realism of *Returning to Haifa,* and it is what continues to make his work so compelling today.

Notes

1. Fawaz Turqi, "Meaning in Palestinian History: Text and Context," *Arab Studies Quarterly* 3, 4 (1981); p. 381.

2. Ghassan Kanafani, "Al-bu'uma fi'l-ghurfa al-ba'ida," in *Maut sarir raqm* 12 (Beirut: Institute for Arab Research, 1980); p. 20.

3. Ghassan Kanafani, Interview in *al-Siyasah* (Kuwait). Cited in Stefan Wild, *Ghassan Kanafani: The Life of a Palestinian* (Wiesbaden: Otto Harrassowitz, 1975), p. 13.

4. Ann Lesch, "The Palestine Arab Nationalism Movement Under the Mandate," in *The Politics of Palestinian Nationalism,* edited by William Quandt (Los Angeles: University of California Press, 1973), pp. 19–20.

5. In two climactic passages of *Returning to Haifa,* Kanafani uses the word *irtitam,* a term that has provided many hours of unresolved discussion with experts as to its exact meaning as well as Kanafani's intent. In context it can best be translated as "collision" or "clash," and it seems to be a way of effecting a sense of inevitability in the confrontation between past and present. Its very ambiguity conveys the manner in which this conflict is internalized in Kanafani's protagonists.

6. Radwa Ashur, *The Way to the Other Tent* [Arabic] [Beirut: Dar al-Adab, 1981), p. 139. This contrasts with Mansur's interpretation that the "abandoned" child represents a Palestine seized by force and given no choice, neither with respect to its fate at that time nor with respect to its present character as a result. Mansur, 220. Ashur's analysis would seem to be borne out by the fact that in the fourth and fifth chapters of the novel Kanafani several times uses the second person plural (Arabic has a singular, dual, and plural in the second person), a device that denotes that the speaker is addressing his statements rhetorically to the Palestinian community in general rather than to the one or two specific individuals.

7. Edward W. Said, *After the Last Sky* (New York: Random House, 1986), p. 38.

8. "An Interview Published for the First Time: With the Martyr Ghassan Kanafani" [Arabic], *Palestinian Affairs* 35 (July 1974): pp. 137–138. [Hereafter referred to as "An Interview."]

9. Ashur, p. 145.

10. Ibid., pp. 145–146.

11. F. Mansur, "Ghassan Kanafani in his Eleven Books" [Arabic], *Palestinian Affairs* 13 (September 1972): p. 220.

12. Ashur, pp. 178–179.

13. "An Interview," p. 138.

14. Ibid., pp. 137, 139.

15. Fadl al-Naqib, *Thus Stories End, Thus They Begin* [Arabic] (Beirut: Muassat al-Abhath al-Arabiyya, 1983), p. 27 [emphasis added].

16. Mansur, p. 220.

PALESTINE'S
CHILDREN

✗

RETURNING TO HAIFA & Other Stories

The Slope

MUHSIN WALKED WITH SLOW HESITATING steps along the corridor leading to his classroom. This was to be his first experience in the world of teaching and he did not see why he had to go in just then. He was doing his utmost to postpone the moment as long as possible.

He had spent the night before tossing and turning in his bed until morning thinking about one thing: how hard it was for someone to stand up in front of people . . . and for what? To teach them! Who do you think you are? he asked himself. You've spent your miserable life without anyone teaching you anything useful. Do you really think you have anything to teach others? You, of all people, who have always believed that school was the last place where a man learns about life? And now you're going to be a schoolteacher?

In the morning he dragged himself off to the principal's office where he sat listening to the other teachers discussing much the same question, only it was from another point of view . . .

"What are we supposed to do in this class when the children have no books?"

The principal's reply was short and even disdainful: "A qualified teacher knows how to conduct his class without books!" Then he added nastily: "Just ask one of the children to take care of the class for you if you can't do it yourself."

Muhsin thought to himself: "It seems this principal wants to give his teachers a lesson in discipline and obedience right from the start. He's had our salaries for a week and now he wants to get our souls as well." He gulped down his tea and stood up . . .

The long corridor was filled with the shouts and clamor of children. It seemed to Muhsin, with his heavy steps, that he was moving through an eddying whirlpool leading him into a meaningless future, a future of nothing but more noise and more nonsense.

"I have a good story, teacher! . . ." This was shouted out by a child slumped in one of the last seats who saw the confusion as a likely opportunity to tell his story. And before Muhsin could even object to the suggestion the child had left his seat and was facing his comrades. He was wearing short pants that were far too large for him and a shirt made out of old material, the kind women wear. His thick black hair hung down to his eyebrows.

"My father was a good man. His hair was white and he had only one eye. His other eye he had poked out himself one day when he was stitching the thick sole of a heavy man's shoe. He was trying hard to get the big needle into the leather, but the sole was very tough. He pushed on the needle with everything he had in him, but no luck. He pushed harder and still it didn't go. Then he put the shoe to his chest and pushed with all his might. All of a sudden the needle went through one side and out the other straight into his eye.

"My father was a good man. He didn't have a long beard, but then it wasn't so short either. He worked very hard and he was good at his work. He always had a lot of shoes to repair and make like new.

"But my father didn't own his own repair shop and there was no one to help him in his work. His shop was really not much more than a box made out of wood and sheet metal and cardboard. There was hardly even enough room for him, some nails, and the shoes and the anvil. Any more and there wouldn't even be room for a fly. If a customer wants his shoes repaired he has to wait outside the shop . . .

"The shop was on the side of a hill, and at the top of the hill was the palace of a rich man. No one who looked for the shop from the balcony of this rich man's palace would be able to see that it was there, because there were plants growing all along the ground. And so my father was not afraid that the owner of the palace would discover his hiding place and make him leave. The rich man never left his palace. His servants took care of bringing everything he wanted to the palace. They all agreed that they would keep my father's secret from their master on the condition that he would repair their shoes in return.

"So my father went on about his work and wasn't afraid. People found out that he could repair shoes so well that they came out looking like new. More and more shoes were brought to him every day. He worked without stopping all day and half the night. And then he said to my mother: 'Tomorrow the children are going to go to school.' To which my mother answered: 'Then you'll rest a little from all this work.'"

When the child went back to his seat, his comrades sat absolutely still, so Muhsin asked: "Why don't you clap for your friend? Didn't you like his story?"

"We want to hear the rest of it . . ."

"Is there any more to your story?"

"A month ago or maybe more it got to be that my father had so much work piled up that he couldn't even come home any more. My mother told us that he was working night and day and couldn't leave his shop. He had no time to go out. Meanwhile the rich man sat on his balcony all day long and all night eating bananas and oranges and almonds and walnuts and throwing away the peels and shells. He threw them over the rails of the balcony of his palace and onto the side of the hill. One morning the hillside was so covered with all these peels and shells that the servants couldn't even find my father's box in the middle of all of them. My mother says that he was so absorbed in his work that he never even noticed all the stuff that was thrown on top of his box. He worked just as he always did. Probably he is still sitting in his box, working away at repairing all the shoes he has so that he can finish them on time and go home. But what I think is that he died there."

The pupils all clapped when the child returned to his seat, where he sat quietly. Sixty staring eyes, a twinkle, but Muhsin . . .

Muhsin took the child to the principal's office, and on the way there he asked him: "Do you really think your father is dead?"

"My father didn't die. I only said that so that the story would end. If I didn't, it would never end. Summer is coming in a couple of months and the sun will dry up all the piles of peels and shells, so they won't be so heavy and then my father can move them away from on top of him and go back to the house."

When Muhsin reached the principal's office he said to him: "I have a genius in my class. He's incredible. Ask him to tell you the story of his father . . ."

"What's your father's story?"

"His shop is very small and he is very skillful. One day his fame reached the owner of the palace that looks out over his little shop, and the rich man sent my father all the old shoes he had and told my father to repair them and make them like new again. All the servants set to work carrying the shoes to the little shop. They worked for two whole days, and when they had finished bringing all the shoes, my father was completely smothered under the huge pile and there was not enough room in the shop for all the shoes . . ."

The principal put his thumbs in his vest pockets, reflected a moment, and said: "This child is crazy. We had better send him to another school."

The child said: "But I'm not crazy. Just go to the rich man's palace and look at his shoes and you'll find little pieces of my father's flesh on them. Maybe you'll even find his eyes and his nose in the sole of one of the shoes . . . Just go there . . ."

The principal interrupted: "In my opinion this child is crazy."

Muhsin answered him: "He's not crazy. I myself used to

bring my shoes to his father's to be repaired. The last time I went, they told me he was dead."

"How did he die?"

"He was pounding the sole of an old shoe. One day he pounded a great many nails into an old shoe to make it absolutely firm. When he had finished he found that he had nailed his fingers between the shoe and the anvil. Just imagine! He was so strong that he could pound a nail through an anvil. But when he tried to get up, he couldn't. He was stuck right to the anvil. The passers-by refused to help him and he remained there until he died."

The principal looked again at Muhsin, who was standing beside the child, one next to the other as if they were one. He shook his head several times without saying anything. Then he went back and sat down in his soft leather chair and began to leaf through his papers, looking from time to time out of the corner of his eye at Muhsin and the child.

—translated by Barbara Harlow

Paper from Ramleh

TWO DIVISIONS OF JEWISH SOLDIERS HALTED US at the side of the road which leads from Ramleh to Jerusalem. They ordered us to raise our hands in the air and cross them. When one of the soldiers noticed that my mother wanted to put me in front of her so that her shadow would protect me from the July sun, he dragged me roughly from her hands and ordered me to stand on one leg with my arms crossed above my head in the middle of the dusty street.

I was nine years old that day. Only four hours before I had seen the Jewish soldiers enter Ramleh. Now, standing there in the middle of the ash-grey road, I watched the Jews look over the jewelry of the old women and the young girls, and then brutally snatch it from them. The tanned female recruits began to do the same thing, but even more enthusiastically. I saw too how my mother looked in my direction, crying silently, and I wanted at that moment to be able to tell her that I was alright, that the sun didn't bother me, in such a way that she would understand . . .

I was one of the ones she still had left. My father had died a full year before the onset of these events. My older brother they took when they first entered Ramleh. I didn't really know what I

37

meant to my mother, but I could imagine now what would happen if I wasn't with her when we reached Damascus, to sell the morning papers, shivering in the cold, near the bus stations.

The sun was beginning to melt the stamina of the women and old men, and from here and there cries of anguish and desperation arose. I saw faces I was used to seeing in the narrow streets of Ramleh, but which now wore the signs of unmitigated sorrow. Never will I be able to explain the strange feeling that came over me when I saw a female Jewish recruit mockingly pull the beard of Uncle Abu Uthman . . .

Uncle Abu Uthman wasn't really my uncle. He was Ramleh's barber and its unassuming doctor. We had got into the habit of loving him ever since we knew him. We called him "uncle" out of respect and esteem. Standing upright now, he held his youngest daughter at his side. Fatima. Small and brown, she looked with her wide black eyes at the female Jewish recruit . . .

"Is she your daughter?"

Abu Uthman shook his head nervously, but his eyes flashed a startling black prophecy. The female recruit simply raised her small gun and aimed it at Fatima's head. The little brown girl with still wondering black eyes . . .

Just at that instant one of the Jewish patrol moved in front of me. The situation had attracted his attention. He stood concealing the scene from me, but I heard the sound of three separate shots. Then he moved and I saw the face of Abu Uthman fill with grief. I looked at Fatima. Her head was hanging forward and blood dripped from her black hair to the warm brown earth.

A little while afterwards Abu Uthman passed by me. He was carrying in his aged arms the small, brown body of Fatima. Rigid and silent, he looked straight ahead with a terrible quietness and hurried past without even glancing at me. I watched his stooped back as he passed silently through the rows of soldiers towards the first narrow street. I kept looking at his wife who was sitting on the ground with her head in her hands crying. At her moans of grief a Jewish soldier turned to her and ordered her to stop. But the old woman didn't stop. She was beyond the limits of despair . . .

Now I could see clearly everything that happened. With my own eyes I saw the way the soldier kicked her with his foot and how the old woman, her face bleeding, fell on her back. All too clearly I saw him thrust the barrel of his rifle at her chest. One shot rang out . . .

The next instant the same soldier turned towards me. Calmly he ordered me to raise my leg which I had lowered again, without noticing, to the ground. Then, when I had raised my leg, he slapped my face twice. With my shirt, he wiped the blood from my mouth from the back of his hand. Helpless as I felt, I looked at my mother standing among the women, her arms raised in the air, crying silently. But just at that moment, through her weeping, there came a small, tearful laugh. I felt my leg twist under my weight and almost give way from the excru-ciating pain. Even so, I laughed too. I wanted to be able one more time to rush to my mother and tell her that the two slaps hadn't hurt very much at all and that I was alright. I wanted her not to cry and to behave the way Abu Uthman had just behaved.

But my thoughts were interrupted when Abu Uthman passed in front of me on his way back to his place after burying Fatima. When he was just opposite me, and even though he didn't look at me at all, I remembered that they had just killed his wife, and that now he was going to have to face still another grief. I watched him in pity, fearful of something, until he had reached his place where he stood for awhile with his back turned. It was hunched and soaked with sweat. But I could imagine his face anyway: frozen, silent, and dotted with shiny beads of perspiration. Abu Uthman stooped down to pick up in his two aged arms the body of his wife. How often I had seen her sitting cross-legged in front of his shop watching him finish his lunch, so she could take the empty dishes home again. It was not long before he walked past me, for the third time, breathing long and heavily, the beads of sweat still shining on his lined face. He was directly opposite me, but didn't look at me at all. Once again I watched his hunched back soaked in sweat as he walked slowly between the rows of soldiers.

The people held back their tears.

A painful silence settled on the women and old men.

It was as if the memories of Abu Uthman were eating persistently away inside the people, all those little remembered stories which Abu Uthman used to tell to the men of Ramleh when they came and sat in his barber's chair . . . memories, each of which seemed to be eating remorselessly away at all the people here.

His whole life Abu Uthman had been a gentle and loving man. He believed in everything, but most of all he believed in himself. He had built his life from nothing. When the revolt in Jabal al-Nar cast him into Ramleh, he lost everything. So he began anew, just as friendly as any plant in the good earth of Ramleh. He won the love and approval of the people. When the last Palestine war began, he sold everything and bought weapons, which he distributed among his relatives so that they would be able to fight in the battle. His shop was transformed into a depot for explosives and arms and he wouldn't take any payment for his sacrifice. The only thing he asked was that he be buried in the beautiful Ramleh cemetery filled with its large trees. This was all he wanted from the people, and all the men of Ramleh knew that Abu Uthman wanted nothing but to be buried in the Ramleh cemetery when he died.

It was these small things which brought silence to the people. Their perspiring faces were heavy with these memories . . . I looked at my mother standing there, her arms raised in the air. She was standing erect, as if she had stopped now, leaden, following Abu Uthman with her quiet eyes. I continued looking into the distance, where I saw Abu Uthman standing in front of a Jewish soldier, talking to him and pointing towards his store. Then he walked alone in the direction of the store. He returned carrying a white towel in which he wrapped the body of his wife . . . then he took the road to the cemetery.

I next saw him from a distance coming back with slow heavy steps. His back was bent and his arms hung helplessly at his sides. He drew slowly near me, walking, older now than he had been before. He was covered with dust and breathing heavily. On his chest were drops of blood mixed with dust . . .

When he was directly opposite me, he looked at me, as if it

were for the first time that he were passing by and seeing me standing there in the middle of the road under the blazing July sun, dusty and soaked in sweat. His lip was hurt and there was blood coming from it. Breathing hard he continued to look at me. There were in his eyes many meanings that I didn't understand but rather felt instead. Then he went on his way, quiet, dusty, and breathing heavily. He stopped, turned his face to the street and raised his arms in the air and crossed them.

The people could no longer bury Abu Uthman as he had wanted. When he went to the mayor's office to confess what he knew, the people heard a dreadful explosion that demolished the whole building. The remains of Abu Uthman were lost amongst the rubble.

They told my mother, while she was carrying me across the hills to Jordan, that when Abu Uthman went to his store before burying his wife, he did not return with only a white towel.

—translated by Barbara Harlow

A Present
for the Holiday

I WAS SLEEPING VERY LATE. THERE IS A CHINESE
writer whose name is Sun Tsi and who lived hundreds of
years before Christ. I was very attracted by him. He relieved
my weariness and held my attention. (However, all that is beside
the point of what I am going to write about.) He wrote that war
is subterfuge and that victory is in anticipating everything and
making your enemy expect nothing. He wrote that war is surprise. He wrote that war is an attack on ideals. He wrote . . .

But all that is beside the point . . .

I was sleeping very late and the telephone rang very early.
The voice that came from the other end was completely
refreshed and awake, almost joyful and proud. There were no
feelings of guilt in its modulations. Half asleep, I said to myself:
this is a man who gets up early. Nothing troubles him at night.
The night had been rainy, with thunder and strong winds. Do
you see what men do in times like this, the men who are march-
ing in the early darkness to build for us an honor unstained by
the mud? The night was rainy, and this man, at the other end of
the line . . .

But all this is also beside the point.

He said to me: "I have an idea. We'll collect toys for the children and send them to the refugees in Jordan, to the camps. You know, these are holidays now."

I was half asleep. The camps. Those stains on the forehead of our weary morning, lacerations brandished like flags of defeat, billowing by chance above the plains of mud and dust and compassion. I had been teaching that day in one of those camps. One of the young students, called Darwish, sold cakes after school was out and I had chased him in between the tents and the mud and the sheets of tin and the puddles in order to get him into the evening class. His hair was short and curly and always wet. He was very bright and he wrote the best creative compositions in the class. If he had found something for himself to eat that day, his genius knew no bounds. It was a big camp. They called it . . .

But that too is beside the point.

The man at the other end of the line said to me: "It's an excellent idea, don't you think? You'll help us. We want a news campaign in the papers, you know." Even though I was half asleep, just the right phrases leapt to mind: "Mr. So-and-So spent his New Year holiday collecting toys for the refugees. High society women will distribute them in the camps." The camps are muddy, and dresses this season are short and the boots are white. Just yesterday I had torn up a news story and photo: the lovely Miss So-and-So spent the evening in such-and-such a nightclub. The young man sitting with her spilled his drink on her dress and she emptied a bottle on his suit. I said, that must have cost at least a hundred pounds. I said, at that price . . .

But all this is beside the point.

Going on, he said to me: "We'll put them in cardboard boxes and find trucks to bring them free of charge. We'll distribute them sealed and that way it will be a surprise." A surprise. War is surprise too. That's what the Chinese writer Sun Tsi said five hundred years before Christ. I was half asleep and I couldn't control this folly. Such accidents occasionally happen to me, especially when I'm tired, and then I can't believe my eyes. I look at people and ask: are these really our faces? All this mud that June has vomited on to them, how could we have cleaned it off so quickly? Can we really be smiling? Is it true? . . .

But this, too, is beside the point.

As the telephone receiver slipped from my hand, he said: "On the morning of the holiday, every child will get a sealed package, with a surprise toy inside it. It will be luck." The receiver fell. The pillow carried me back nineteen years.

It was the year 1949.

They told us that day: the Red Cross will bring all you children presents for the holiday. I was wearing short pants and a gray cotton shirt and open shoes without socks. The winter was the worst the region had ever seen and when I set out that morning my fingers froze and were covered with something like fine glass. I sat down on the pavement and began to cry. Then a man came by and carried me to a nearby shop where they were lighting a wood fire in some kind of tin container. They brought me close and I stretched my feet towards the flame. Then I went racing to the Red Cross Centre, and stood with the hundreds of children, all of us waiting for our turn.

The boxes seemed very far away and we were trembling like a field of sugar cane and hopping about in order to keep the blood flowing in our veins. After a million years, my turn came. A clean starched nurse gave me a red square box.

I ran "home" without opening it. Now, nineteen years later, I have completely forgotten what was in that dream box. Except for just one thing: a can of lentil soup.

I clutched the soup can with my two hands red from the cold and pressed it to my chest in front of ten other children, my brothers and relatives, who looked at it with their twenty wide eyes.

Probably the box held splendid children's toys too, but these weren't to eat and so I didn't pay any attention to them and they got lost. I kept the can of soup for a week, and every day I gave my mother some of it in a water glass so she could cook it for us.

I remember nothing except the cold, and the ice that manacled my fingers, and the can of soup.

The voice of the man who wakes up early was still ringing in my head that tired gray morning when the bells began to clang in a dreadful emptiness. I returned from my trip into the past which continued to throb in my head, and I . . .

But all of that too is beside the point.

—translated by Barbara Harlow

The Child Borrows
His Uncle's Gun
and Goes East to Safad

E LEANED HIS WET BACK AGAINST THE ROCK and stretched out his legs in relaxation, looking up at the sky. Dark clouds, their edges incandescent in the sunlight as if aflame, fought with each other above his head. A heavy silence hung all around him. Not once had it occurred to him that such rugged terrain as this might actually exist. When his uncle had told him that the path from Majd al-Kurum to Safad was difficult even for goats, he hadn't believed him. Smiling quietly, he had just stretched out his hand and taken the ancient Turkish gun. While he stood there clutching it to his chest, his uncle had repeated to him once more: "The path between Majd al-Kurum and Safad is so rocky that even the goats find it difficult. A child like you will die in the thorns before he gets halfway there."

Without looking at his uncle, he repeated for the tenth time that morning that the word "child" which his uncle kept insisting on using did not apply to him: "I'm not a child."

"You're seventeen years old and the gun you're carrying weighs more than half as much as you do. And the way is long and fierce."

Fear overcame him for just a moment, but he held the gun even tighter to his chest and turning around he stood face to face with his uncle again: "If you're worried about your gun, why don't you just say so?"

"It's you I'm worried about. Even though you're a crazy kid, I don't want to discourage you. Why don't you stand out on the road and catch a car that will take you to Safad? Why do you want to go to Safad anyway? Are there so few men there?"

His uncle didn't really seem to want an answer to all these questions, since when he finished talking he stretched out his hand and patted his shoulder, thus putting an end to the conversation which had been going on for an hour or more. "Farewell. Watch out that this beast of a cannon you're carrying doesn't go bad on you. Don't put too much faith in it. It's pretty old, but it still works."

What a strange uncle this is who gives things all different names, who says "child" to him instead of calling him by his own name, and who refers to the old rifle as a "cannon." He must really know more things than any other creature on the face of the earth. When he had knocked at his door early that morning hoping to borrow his gun, his uncle hadn't hesitated even for a single minute, but then he had spent over an hour warning him about the path and its savageness. His warning was absolutely right though. The day was half gone and he was still only halfway there. Now he was afraid that he wouldn't get to Safad until it was dark. If he got there at all!

Last night's rain had soaked the soil and washed the desolate mountain rocks. Even so it had still looked dry when his mother saw him slip out of the door of the house at dawn. She didn't ask where he was going, but just told him to put on his overcoat. There was no discussion. Did she know somehow about his plan that he had been chewing over by himself for three days now?

A quarter of an hour later an old bus on its way from Acre came by. He squeezed himself in among the crowd of silent passengers all bundled in their overcoats and handed his last two piasters to the driver who put them in his pocket without even looking at them. When he got out at the Nahaf intersection, the other passengers just stared at him with their silent eyes. The sun was shining weakly by the time he began to climb the dusty road separating Nahaf from the main thoroughfare but the mountain frost still cut him harshly to the bones.

He pounded with his fist on the wooden door of his Uncle Abu al-Hassan's house, knowing that his uncle would have finished the dawn prayer and returned to his bed to get some more sleep. It was a habit of his that hadn't changed for as long as he could remember his uncle and his uncle's house. The door opened and two surprised eyes wished him good morning. Even before entering, he blurted out his brief story: "The men in Safad are surrounding the citadel and I came to borrow your gun so I can go there. Will you give it to me?"

"And where are you going to get the cartridges?"

"I bought them."

"How many did you get?"

"About twenty."

"And so with twenty cartridges you're going to storm the citadel in Safad?"

"Will you give me the gun? I'll bring it back in two days."

"And what if you get killed?"

His uncle was smiling when he said this, as if he didn't really believe the story anyway. His nephew, however, didn't smile back, nor did he hesitate in answering all these questions: "If I die, Hisam will return it to you. I know he's there and I'll get him to do it."

His uncle turned on his heels. Stepping inside, he disappeared down the passageway, where his voice was heard calling: "Come in, child, and have some breakfast."

But he didn't go in—that much he had decided from the beginning—and shouted instead: "Are you going to give me the gun?"

"Did you dream all this up at night? Hadn't you better call now on the Provider and Omniscient One?"

"I want to know if you'll lend me your gun, not waste time, because if you won't lend it to me, then I have to go right away to Kisra. Abu Mustafa has another gun and he may let me borrow it."

Several long minutes had passed in silence when his uncle reappeared at the end of the passage and began looking him over carefully. The old man was tall and the years had not narrowed his shoulders. He bared his arms covered with thick graying hair and placed an embroidered skullcap on his short white hair. Another minute passed in which they exchanged looks, as if it were some kind of examination. Then came the question he had been waiting for: "Have you told this story to the old woman?"

"My mother does not like being called an old woman."

He smiled. His uncle, however, repeated his question. His frown showed that the joke had been unintended: "The old woman, does she know what her son is planning?"

A sudden happiness came over him as he realized, much to his surprise, that he was serious and that his uncle was not just going over the details. This meant that, when all was said and done, he would get the gun.

He took off his shoes and walked in, while his uncle made way for him in the passage which he had been blocking with his arms. He looked at him with his narrow eyes as he entered the room furnished with woollen carpets and cushions of straw. When he had sat down his uncle shook his head sorrowfully. He had given up expecting an answer, and it was not long before he came to a decision.

"Umm al-Hassan is making tea. Don't tell her anything. I'll give you the cannon."

"I knew you would."

"You're taking advantage of the kindness of your uncle's heart, but you're a mischievous child . . . Where did you buy the cartridges?"

"In Majd al-Kurum."

"How much did you pay?"

"A pound and a half."

"Where did you get it?"

"Legally, you know, every single piastre."

"Anyway, stolen bullets can kill just as well."

The gun was under the bed, as he well knew. Nearly every Friday for four years his uncle had allowed him to shoot it, just one or two bullets, out in the field. Afterwards it was cleaned and oiled and hidden under the bed again.

It was a heavy rifle, but he carried it lightly without even noticing. When his uncle had opened the door for him, softly so that Umm al-Hassan wouldn't see him, he slung it to his shoulder. He walked slowly at first, but soon moved faster until he was almost running. He turned east and climbed over the few rocks in the fields that obstructed him. Then he began to strike the really rugged terrain. His uncle had told him to keep out of the way of the fields of the settlements at Rameh which he would run right into on the road. But if he kept going east and just slightly north he would meet only Arab villages and then come to the valleys around Safad.

He walked half the day and the gun began to weigh heavier and heavier on his shoulder and kept banging mercilessly against his thigh. He decided to rest awhile and leaned his back against a rock at the side of the narrow path that had been dug out by men's feet in a short cut over the hills. He felt the muscles in his legs snap and once again was taken by a sudden fear. But the gun was there, resting on his legs, like some legendary thing, quiet and unknown, awakened in the heart of man.

"Anyway, it's better than losing the gun." He said this out loud, just to give himself confidence. "The easy road is full of English patrols. If they ever saw me with a gun, they'd take it away."

He stroked the gun's stock and smiled weakly: "The piastres went for cartridges . . . you know that."

He stood the gun up in front of him with its butt fixed between his feet and continued pushing it with both hands into the moist ground. He pulled his hands back greedily and joined them together behind his head. He leaned back against the rock, looking at the gun.

"Soon I'll get a special rifle. It will be only mine and you'll go back to your house under the woollen mattress. If they let you out, it will only be to hunt birds and squirrels, maybe sometimes foxes, but only sometimes."

The gun had a long barrel but the opening at the end was missing its pin. Its leather strap was broken and in place of it his uncle had attached a fibre rope moistened with oil which blackened his hands, already dirty from working in the soil year after year, giving them a heavy, dark color. The firing chamber took only one cartridge which was loaded from an opening on the side. He didn't know, however, if the rifle was originally made like this or if it hadn't simply ended up this way with the passing of time. Probably instead of it taking a cartridge clip of five or six cartridges, you had to remove the breech, first from on top, then from behind, so that you dropped one cartridge after another into the firing chamber, or something like that, which was no longer there. Maybe it was just a matter of working out the original form of this rifle from experts specializing in the history of weapons and arms. His uncle probably treated this gun the way he treated the trees in his little field, trimming the roots and stripping off the branches in order to graft on new ones, raising and pruning and filling in the gaps, until the whole thing seemed to have been made over. You see what he did with this rifle in the last quarter of a century. Maybe this had something to do with why he called it a cannon, but for whatever reason it had lost most of the distinguishing characteristics of a rifle. It sounded like thunder when you fired it.

"Even so, you're a good rifle . . . and your aim almost never misses. The important thing is that you're faithful. And your bullets come out of only one place. I hope."

The rifle stock was a dark brown color and seemed to be made in one piece. Except that it wasn't. Once he had seen his uncle patch the stock with a piece of olive wood which, after sawing and sanding it with unbelievable care, he had nailed with real first-rate skill to the stock. The piece of the stock had been damaged one day when his uncle had been obliged to use the butt of his rifle to kill an adder that had surprised him on the way home. That day he crushed the adder's head and part of his rifle stock at the same time. The incident couldn't have made Abu al-Hassan very happy, since it had almost put an end to the life of the rifle.

"If I wanted to own a gun of my own, why did I borrow you from Uncle Abu al-Hassan? You better be really good with me if you want me to borrow you again. Strange, isn't it? I mean that I went from Majd al-Kurum to Nahaf just to borrow a gun so I could go and fight in Safad . . . of course, Abu Mustafa has a rifle in Kisra, a good rifle, with a cartridge clip and a strip and everything a rifle is supposed to have to make it a good weapon. Only Abu Mustafa wouldn't lend it to me. Anyway, Kisra isn't on the way from Majd al-Kurum to Safad, but even so it would have been worth going out of the way for . . ."

Less than a minute later he was standing up. He grabbed the gun and struck out quickly along the valley towards the east: "Damn imagination. Damn daydreams," as the professor once said.

He tried to think of the professor, but then shook his head violently, driving the thought away. He slung his gun to his shoulder, and tightening his fist around the bullets in his pants pocket, began to hurry. The sun was already directly overhead, although hidden by clouds thickening under it like balls of cotton.

"So with twenty cartridges you're going to attack the citadel at Safad."

He repeated his uncle's mocking sentence which kept coming back into his mind. He pushed back a bunch of boxthorn with his hand and started to climb over a pile of stones that was blocking the way. All the while he was thinking: "If every man in Galilee took twenty cartridges and went to the citadel in Safad, we'd smash it to pieces in a minute." He picked his way carefully down the pile of rocks. His legs were tight and he was clutching the gun in his hand behind his back. He held it away from his body in order to keep his balance.

"It takes a lot of effort. And leadership. Just like the hajj said." For a few moments he tried to imagine what this word meant. Leadership. But he didn't get anywhere. First of all, he imagined that the importance of the leader must be to go around to all the fighters one by one and guide them in what they had to do. But he got rid of this image: "All that is just a lot of empty talk. It's not simple." When he had still further weakened the image by adding details he ended by getting rid of the thought altogether, and started instead to calculate how many hours he still had left in these rocks. "It must be six or seven." He thought of resting again, but then decided to keep going.

His father and mother were waiting for him to come and have lunch. Today was Friday and prayer time was already several hours ago. On Friday he usually ate lunch with his parents. They would miss him. Then his father would begin to eat, saying while he chewed his first mouthful: "While your heart worries about your son, your son worries about the rock. This troublesome child . . ."

His mother would hesitate for a moment before her sixth sense would begin to vex her, or her afreet, as she used to like to say, begin to whisper in her ear things that made her worry. Even so she concealed this from her husband, and reached stoically towards her food. Observing her out of the corner of his eye, he would say to her: "Do you suppose he's not going to eat now? Eh? Or do you think he's reaching for his food right now with his hand just like you're doing? I swear on my father's bones that he's gobbling up his lunch with both hands in some fiery hell and filling his gullet without giving us a moment's thought."

His mother wouldn't resist, but would just go on eating as if what had just been said had nothing at all to do with her. It was her habit, whenever something bothered her deeply, to turn her thoughts to something else.

To the west, about an hour away by car, was Acre. Then a little to the south from there lay Haifa, where her oldest son lived and worked in King Faisal Street. His office was in the two outer rooms of a magnificent second floor apartment, and he himself lived alone in the two inner rooms. He wasn't married yet. Just so that people would one day call him "Doctor," his father had sold a section of olive trees and each year set aside a certain number of containers of olive oil which were then sold in order to defray the cost of books and microscopes for Doctor Qassim.

In spite of the father's contempt, the son did well. One day he returned from Beirut, and the first thing he did when he met his father who had gone to welcome him in Acre was to stick out his tongue as far as he could right in his face. "Is this what you learned from the Americans in Beirut, you rude child?"

Qassim, who had been preparing his answer all along the way, replied: "Of Course not. I studied medicine and now I'm a doctor. A doctor through and through, even though you spent all these years telling me how impossible it was and that I was such a disappointing child, and that I was going to study a thousand years and then come back and be a farmer!"

His father couldn't repress the happiness that was overflowing inside him. He took his son by the arm and pushed him towards an ancient Ford, which he had made a down-payment on that morning just to transport the two of them, the suitcases and the books to Majd al-Kurum, where Umm Qassim had stuffed three chickens, a neck and some tripe. She gathered the family and the food and they all went out half the way to meet the beloved returnee.

"Hey, Doctor Qassim. Ten years ago you learned in the elementary reader that . . ."

Qassim, laughing, cut him off. "A donkey is a donkey, even when he's been brought up with horses. That's what you always said to me when I told you I was going to be a doctor. Well, the donkeys and the horses are going to stay in Majd al-Kurum and your obedient servant is going to open an office in Haifa."

Just as quickly as the joy which had filled his chest, anger now mounted to the forehead of Abu Qassim: "Haifa? Are there so few doctors in Haifa?"

"Where do you want me to work then?"

"In Majd al-Kurum, you useless son."

"In Majd al-Kurum? Do you think I'm the kind of doctor who treats his patients with leeches? No one in Majd al-Kurum will pay more than a penny. Do you want me to die of hunger?"

Abu Qassim pressed his lips tightly together. The matter was finished—finished all the moments of joy. He knew well enough that if he continued the conversation, he would only come out with something disagreeable to the son who had just arrived from another world. He didn't want his son to see the lump of fear he felt in his throat for one moment of weakness, so he stared out the car window as the fields of olive trees passed before his eyes, their leaves glistening in the sun like so many small sheets of silver.

"How is mother?"

"Fine."

"And the child?"

"He's in school. This little one loves the fields." His chest relaxed as happiness returned suddenly to him. The fields of olive trees appeared before him bathed in a holy light: "The child loves the fields. As soon as he comes home from school, he plunges straight into the canal up to his knees. He has real farmer's hands . . . He's always sneaking out of the house at night to go and sleep under the olive trees . . ."

Qassim's voice cut him off again. "You're killing this boy . . . You're really killing him, for God's sake! Tomorrow I'm taking him with me to Haifa. He'll learn to make the kind of future he wants."

Abu Qassim wheeled around and grabbed his son by the arm: "Look at the Jews, when one of them sets out to work in the villages . . . Why don't you open your office in Majd al-Kurum?"

But the car had stopped. Just at that moment Abu Qassim saw, with a clarity he would never forget, the look of scorn which flashed in his son's eyes. It lasted no more than a fraction of a second, but he saw it and felt it, like mountains crashing down, fall upon his chest. The next instant the women's trilling had burst forth and the car door opened. Qassim got out and was seized amidst arms and clothes and embroidery. Inside the car, as if nailed to his seat like a stone, Abu Qassim watched his wife press her brown tear-stained face to that of her returning son, moistening it with her tears which were pouring down to her knees, sobbing on his chest while she squeezed him in her arms, which she clasped determinedly about him. All around them trilling announced the deep pride she felt in the man who had gone away a farmer and returned home a doctor: "O my support, my child, my heart. O son of Majd al-Kurum her glory. O return of the knight. Protect him O Guardian, with a hundred hands from the evil eye. O Protector, O adored one!"

While the family solemnly escorted Qassim to the house,

Abu Qassim walked along far behind the boisterous throng. He picked up a stick and began hitting the side of his long belted *qunbaz* with it, producing a tearing-like sound. From where he was, he could see the little one racing behind the crowd trying to grab hold of his big brother who had now returned. He broke the stick, bent it and, throwing it on the ground, began to quicken his steps.

"There's still the child."

—*translated by Barbara Harlow*

Dr. Qassim Talks to Eva About Mansur Who Has Arrived in Safad

FROM HIS POSITION IN THE ROCKING CHAIR IN THE home of Eva's family, Doctor Qassim looked out at the houses of Haifa stacked at the foot of Mount Carmel and the stony field stretching off towards the port. All of it was exposed to the barrel of the gun set up on the roof of the house. He didn't quite recall the details of the story which he had read that morning about the two Arabs who had been killed by bullets from some far-off gun, or whether the incident had occurred near this very region.

He drank his tea quietly trying not to talk too much just for the sake of passing time lest the conversation approach limits which were too uncertain for him. He did not meet Eva's eyes directly nor the eye of the gun which was staring down on him from above. He began to spread a piece of fried bread with butter, coating it with a large spoonful of jam which he then covered with another piece of bread. The whole thing occurred just as he was about to take the first bite. When he raised his head, something appeared in front of him. Through the pale blue mist were the domes and rooftops of Acre. At the same time he remembered Majd al-Kurum. It seemed distant to him, an ambiguous distance not unlike oblivion. He didn't need to go over the matter in all its details, knowing that it was impossible for him to flee the memories which were beginning to reverberate inside his brain. He felt as if there were some terrible danger encircling him, in Haifa, in Acre, in Majd al-Kurum. His father, his mother, his younger brother. As if he could feel it buzzing, he got to his feet impatiently. He knew very well that there was no way for him to avoid submitting to the unknown something which had suddenly overwhelmed him. He put the slice of bread back in the bowl and leaned back in the chair, looking straight ahead without seeing anything in particular.

Even though he could feel Eva's eyes studying him, he was unable to take on any role whatever. When he started to think about Eva, the image became altogether muddled in his mind and the features were lost. He profoundly wanted Eva to stop looking at him as if he were something requiring such minute scrutiny and trembled at the mere thought that she might start talking to him.

The next minute she was doing just that, beginning precisely where he had dreaded she would begin: "Everything has become so complicated. One of these days we should try to look straight in each other's eyes and really see what's the matter."

"Which matter?"

She stretched her arms forward, making a wide circle with her right hand and pointing towards the horizon where her hand passed above the pale domes of Acre, and to the east of Acre over the seemingly level Tel al-Fakhar. In a trembling voice, she answered: "The matter you've been thinking about just now."

He took the slice of bread and passed it to Eva so that it almost touched her face. Little by little he was beginning to recover his nerve.

"At the moment I'm thinking about a much smaller matter . . . Do you see this slice of bread? Well, when I spread the jam on top of the butter, I remembered my little brother . . . He always thought that putting jam on butter was a kind of lack of taste. Either you eat butter or you eat jam, but you can't eat them both together. If you do, then it is an expression of disdain either for the honor of the butter or for the honor of the jam. Anyway my brother believed, and he still does, that butter is a kind of food which contains all the elements which make it valuable in itself and so it shouldn't be underestimated or abused. I need to recover those words because he had been able to express his opinion so simply and clearly. This is what I was thinking about, and I was reminded of it while I was spreading the slice of bread. I thought you would have known that, since it happens to everyone from time to time."

"But you never told me that you had a little brother!"

"He's not exactly little. He's seventeen now, I think. But we've got used to calling him the child."

"You never told me you have a brother."

"There are a lot of things I didn't tell you, and a lot of things that you don't tell me. We make our world smaller with our hands in order to force outside its limits everything that has nothing to do with us. We make it smaller so we can fill it with happiness."

"What does your brother do in the village? Why didn't you bring him here?"

"He's a boy who loves the fields. That's what father always says. He's like a pure-bred horse which can only live in the meadows."

She passed him the slice of bread which he took coldly. In order not to get involved in the matter, he began to eat, but it was without appetite. His brother Mansur was somewhere in the rocky terrain around Safad sprinkling handfuls of rotting wild thyme on half a piece of coarse dark brown bread. He put the other half back in his large pants pocket on top of the cartridges. The butt of the old Turkish gun kept bumping against the back of his leg whenever he was obliged to jump over the rocks.

He moved the gun to his other shoulder where the fibre rope cut a dark brown line on his white shirt. Directly underneath it he could feel something like a wound that had opened at the top of his shoulder which was supporting the full weight of the gun. The rope rubbed like a saw. His uncle must not have thought of this problem. Certainly if he had, he would have come up with a solution of one kind or another. But as a matter of fact his uncle never really needed to hang the heavy gun from his shoulder for such a long distance, and used to just carry it by the middle in his big rough hand, since he never took it far from the house. At the time of his first assignment for it, during the revolt when he had taken it to the mountains, the original leather belt was probably still in good condition.

All of a sudden he saw the road a few metres off and in a matter of seconds he knew exactly where he was. Even though he had been to Safad only two or three times, he could still remember the distinguishing features of the main road leading to it. Without stepping on the asphalt in the middle of the road, he surveyed everything around him, listening closely to every movement, and trying to take in everything all at once.

When he reached the market, his nostrils filled with the smells of vegetables and baskets and early morning rain. People were moving about without taking much notice of the sound of bullets, which gave the atmosphere a feeling of intolerable tension. Quickening his pace, he said to himself: "They're strange, these city people, it's as if the matter didn't even concern them," and he made way for an old car which had begun to careen among the people, cutting them off with its raucous horn. Both sides of the car were splashed with mud and the front window was smashed. There appeared to be bullet holes pocking the hood along a straight line. In one of the holes someone had fixed a flag whose staff was just the size of the hole so that there was no need to attach it with a rope or wire. The flag, which was stitched out of shining clean cloth, began to wave. It fluttered rapidly because of its shortness, making a sound that could be heard over the noise of the engine, the horn, and the four men in the car.

All of a sudden the car cut in front of him. Its roof was chopped off from the middle as if by a saw, giving it a comical shape. It seemed to him to resemble a man without his pants. Inside the car the men had turned the back seat around and were leaning against the front seat. From there they had begun to observe the people. A small space extended in front of their legs the whole of which had been created by the seat and the back trunk of the car whose top had been removed. The space made by sawing off the car's roof was filled with boxes of vegetables and bread and jugs of water.

When the car passed in front of him, one of the three men pointed at him with the end of a long revolver which he had placed on his arm: "So this is the peasant who wants to get through to Safad. Look, he's carrying a stick."

The car was moving very slowly among the crowds of people. The other two men laughed. One of them was carrying a short French rifle. The cartridge clips were slung across his chest. The other man was chewing on something.

"How much did you pay for this stick?"

"Damn you, or else this stick will beat you instead."

He said it quietly, but his voice was agitated. He had felt the sharp insult to himself and his gun and envied the man sitting in the middle with the short French rifle and cartridges of bullets filling his chest. The one with the revolver kept the handle pointed at him as the car slowly pulled away. Then he heard his voice: "If you were a man this would be the place to blow your brains out with just one bullet."

He took his gun from his shoulder and carried it across his chest. There was one bullet ready in the firing chamber. For the first time this old gun seemed to him like something warm and intimate. He shouted with everything he had, so that it would be easy for the man with the revolver to hear him: "If you were a man you'd get down."

Even so, mere words weren't enough and he started to run after the car. Before he had succeeded in grabbing on to something at the back of it, one of the men, the one still chewing, stopped and began to address the other men in the car: "Shame on you ... Shame on you ..."

He turned towards Mansur who was still running behind the car: "Where are you from, brother?"

"Majd al-Kurum."

"What are you doing in Safad with that gun?"

"I heard that you're surrounding the citadel and I came to join you."

"Are you going to surround the citadel?"

He looked at the other two men who had begun to shake

with laughter, then leaned over and lifted one of the boxes on
top of another to make more room.

"Come on up with us. It would be a pretty mean thing for
us to leave you to run behind the car forever."

He reached out his hand for Mansur to grab hold of. Once
he had it, he jumped and landed firmly on the metal floor of
the car. Before he had really even adjusted to his seat, one of the
men offered him a tomato. He was hungry and tired and he felt
strange, but the story of the citadel was eating away at his mind.

"You're not surrounding the citadel?"

"The citadel has been abandoned since Adam was a child."

"What are you doing then?"

"We've been skirmishing in the Jewish quarter."

"What about the citadel?"

"The English would shoot if even a rat moved in it, but
we're in control of it."

He was shocked, he felt so useless. He didn't know anything
and the whole crazy undertaking had been a reckless idea with
no basis to it at all. The car, having left the crowd, had picked
up speed and began to bounce like a rubber ball over the street,
which was filled with holes. The man with the revolver said:
"Get the barrel of this stick away from my face. It could go off if
a fly landed on the hammer . . . I know about this kind of
weapon."

He threw the rest of the tomato into the road and adjusted
himself in his seat, but the man with the revolver kept up his
game: "If we hadn't found him about to occupy the citadel with
his stick, he might have driven us out!"

Mansur thought a bit and decided that the man with the
revolver was a mean creature and that what he had to do was
teach him about means and ends. Quietly he put his gun down
on the boxes of vegetables, and stared him in the face.

"Would you wrestle with me?"

"You're nervous."

"Would you wrestle with me?"

The man with the revolver studied him carefully as he
slumped sharply to the floor of the car. Under his shirt his
shoulders looked round and stiff, and his broad forearms were

like blocks of wood. His hands were as if made of hammered brown steel. He raised his eyes and stared at his face. He was young, with black eyes slightly sunken below his thick eyebrows and sparkling like those of a hyena. A powerful determination radiated from them.

He came simply to a decision and looked at Ustaz Ma'aruf, slapping him with his left hand on the leg.

"A young man like this one doesn't wrestle."

"Then keep quiet."

The man with the revolver persisted in what was supposed to resemble a joke but wasn't one. "So he eats a serpent's head, but this isn't meant to stop us from getting to know him. I'm a realistic man, so easy that a young man like this doesn't wrestle, I openly admit to you, Ustaz Ma'aruf, that he might be able to wrestle and beat me in less than a minute, and this is something that I don't like. If a peasant comes from Majd al-Kurum to your village and challenges you right there in the middle of the village, then he might knock you down."

All of a sudden the car stopped and the driver, who throughout the trip had been paying no attention to his friends, looked around. He was wearing a dirty blue jacket. His beard of some time was neither long nor short and seemed untrimmed so that it gave his face a look of misery. He opened the car door noisily and, without so much as looking at them, announced: "We can't go on. The damned gunfire is blocking the road and I can't trust this car. It's dangerous for the motor to stop and rest. And we're in the middle of the danger zone."

The man with the revolver jumped on top of the boxes and started to laugh: "You always give the same lecture: the gunfire, the damned motor, the road. Don't you think we ever understand? Eh? You just don't believe it."

The driver didn't answer, but turned towards the back of the car. He dragged out the biggest of the boxes and lifted it to his shoulders. Barely hanging on to the sides, he began to climb up the road.

Ustaz Ma'aruf said: "You're going to have to carry a box too, Mansur, and come join us."

"Where to?"

"We're bringing food to the men. They haven't eaten anything since this morning."

Mansur slung the strap of his gun over his shoulder and
picked up a box of soft overripe tomatoes and hurried along
behind Ustaz Ma'aruf.

It was a paved lane extending between the stone walls of the
low houses. Their windows were of minutely worked wood and
were carefully locked. The lane led steeply up the hill, wide at
times and then narrowing until finally there was not space
enough for two men to walk side by side. Each curve seemed
like it must be the end of the lane, but only turned out to be a
deception. Behind the lane, above it, in it, no one knew, there
were the sounds of bullets whistling. Anonymous shots
skimmed the edges of the roofs producing sparks which fell on
the stone rooms. There was an odor of silence and death and
fear and courage and alarm coming from wives who didn't
know if their husbands were still alive.

Mansur caught up with Ustaz Ma'aruf. The carefully painted jug with its curved mouth bounced on top of his box and he
could hear the panting of Ustaz Ma'aruf as he climbed upward
in his heavy black shoes.

"Where are they?"

"Who?"

"The Jews."

"On the roofs, behind the iron windows, where only divine
bullets can penetrate."

"Where are we?"

"You'll see now . . . behind the alleys, in front of every hole
big enough for a fly."

Ustaz Ma'aruf put down his box and placed his hands on
his hips. The driver had reached the end of the lane where a
wide space appeared to extend between the two walls. He put
down his box and moved towards the other two men. The man
with the revolver and the man with the rifle began to look out
from over his shoulder to the open area.

Ustaz Ma'aruf spoke: "They're waiting for an opportunity.
Do you see that little courtyard? Well, there's a bloody rifle
which commands it from the roof of the tallest house in the

Jewish quarter. Yesterday they killed a man. Today they almost killed a child . . . Early this morning they hit three cats."

"Cats?"

"That's right. The man with the rifle seemed to want to make us understand that no one was safe and that his aim was good enough to shoot something even half a kilometre or more away. Cats . . . Probably he put a telescope on his gun."

Ustaz Ma'aruf flapped his pockets. Then he took out a small pen and squatted down on the ground. "Come here so I can explain it to you."

Mansur squatted down next to him and tried to follow the twisted lines which Ustaz Ma'aruf was drawing slowly and carefully on the snow-white tiles.

The Acre road goes eastward and then climbs to the north and goes from there into Safad. It makes a half circle around the green hills of stone and wild thyme. If we say that the center of Safad is the old destroyed citadel on top of the high hill, then it's easy to imagine the countryside. To the west of the citadel is the Kurdish section. From there to the east extends the Jewish quarter on two sides. To the south is the al-Wata section. The market is a small area with a fresh damp aroma which is situated between the al-Wata section, the Jewish quarter, and the area of the citadel. The heavy stone houses there are scattered about like panting attempts to climb the hill, which faces the citadel itself with its heavy arched stones.

West of the citadel stretches the Kurdish quarter with its stone houses coated with plaster. Seen from the citadel, they look like snow-white pigeons with their wings outspread over a carpet of dark green.

The vaulted houses with domes were built from stones taken from the al-Jarmaq quarry. The people of Safad call these superior stones, since they are able to preserve their mountain soul, desolate, coarse and firm, year after year, as if they were still a part of the mountain itself, and not yet dug out of it. You can always get stones from the mountains to build the walls of a house, high or low, rich or poor, but the stones from al-Jarmaq are the only stones whose soul you can't steal, nor can you deprive them of their connections with the mountains. If you build one of them into the neat, upright wall, you can't pass by it without feeling that you're in the mountain air, helpless, dispersed, doomed. But it continues to carry with it its intense longing for the rough rocky terrain, giving off a wild aroma, as if it were still planted in a thicket of thyme.

In Safad, even though there were four thousand Jews who had never, for one day, been farmers, no one minded. They'd lived in their small shops for a long time, selling their wares to the people, exchanging greetings with them and long conversations. They'd be invited to lunch and dinner. Because they'd been there for a long time, they knew how to speak Arabic. They were called by Arabic names and they read Arabic books and newspapers. It seemed logical for the inhabitants of Safad to call them Arab Jews. There would have been no problem if the large shops hadn't started to spring up in the country, surreptitiously, like plants, in the night. They said: The Ashkenazi came and took a closed-off, isolated corner on the side of the Jewish quarter. This happened in such a way that in the beginning no one noticed. The old men then didn't worry much about the matter. Now these store owners are sitting behind their wooden desks in the biggest stores in the country. Take Iskandar. Is there a Safadi who doesn't know the shops of Iskandar which sell lots of small housewares and notions? Or Roshar Braunfeld who sells foodstuffs? Then there's also Yusuf Banderley who specializes in dairy products and cheeses. No one knows where he buys the things that fill his shop which is never closed except on Saturday. Behind a wide glass counter people are always doing business with the foreigner Mr. Bar in his pharmacy with wooden doors. Most people don't know Edel Mayberg personally, but all Safad knows that he is the owner of the Central Hotel which is run anonymously like a number of the small hotels and restaurants.

Edel Mayberg, Edel . . . Edel . . . Who suspects that he's a member of the Haganah? And that his hotels and restaurants and houses are filled with arms? Or the foreigner Mr. Bar, the one who looks out at people from behind the glass counter and whose face looks like a chicken's face, who would bet that he's a military officer who procures weapons and draws up plans?

Banderley . . . Braunfeld . . . They dispatch especially for the future. Everything is perfectly inventoried. Probably this was a surprise not only for the Arabs of Safad but for the old Jews as well. They said so and said so and said so, then they were silent.

Year after year, through its tiled lanes, Safad saw dozens of rabbis approach the synagogues, of which there were three in the town. These old men with their long white beards and round black head coverings, did they know? Did they? You can't say anything now. The English knew. This is true and that much you can say with confidence. They came with weapons. Lots and lots of weapons, light, medium, and heavy. How is it that the English found hunting cartridges with us, and didn't find all these weapons with them? Look at them now. They let them shoot. But if we so much as shoot one bullet, Mr. Birham, the police chief, comes with his men in cars and on horseback to harry our rearguard with bullets and whips. When they could, they let them climb up to the citadel from time to time. What are they doing there? Only Mr. Birham knows. Are they mounting a cannon? Or digging a trench? Or burying machine guns? Can't anyone say? Mr. Birham is the only one who knows. But if we try to go there to see what they're doing, we just find armed English behind every stone. Armed English, one in front of another, who tell you: Go away!

It was an ignoble fight. Two days ago, Edel Mayberg and his son opened fire on Safad for an hour. From where? From that very citadel. The English were in their beds sound asleep in the Mount Canaan Centre and in the home of Hajj Fu'ad al-Kholy which they had made into another center for themselves between the Kurdish and the Jewish quarters, and in the central police station in the al-Wata quarter. For a whole hour of shooting not one of them woke up. But then when our young men began to climb the road to the citadel, they all got up and went racing off without even putting their pants on. An ignoble fight, like trying to stop an armored car with your bare hands.

Ustaz Ma'aruf's hands were also bare. His short pen moved in a circle over the tiles leaving twisting lines. Over and over until the tiles were transformed into thick lead lines with no beginning and no end, while the pen went on drawing. In the still remaining clear space between the intertwining lines was placed one round dot.

"We are here now. Between us and the Jewish quarter there's a row of British who are following us like police dogs. That's why we're not stopping in any fixed places. It wouldn't be too smart. That empty courtyard there in front of you belongs to the Central Hotel, the hotel of Edel Mayberg and his son. The British are blind to everything as far as we're concerned . . . do you understand anything of all this? Here we are like one man sitting on the roof of a minaret fighting an entire city. The bullets come at him from every side. But actually this example isn't quite right. Let's change it to an upside-down minaret, or the devil's own well surrounded by a thousand springs . . . do you understand this? What brought you here from Majd al-Kurum anyway? Are there so few men in Safad?"

The question came as a surprise. As if he had been talking to some other man right by the pavement, Ustaz Ma'aruf hadn't even raised his head. The pen continued to give off a sharp screeching sound as it moved about above the dark black dot shiny as pitch. Mansur decided not to answer, since in fact he didn't know the answer. Once more he took refuge in the world he had quietly regulated in his own mind. He decided again that a question of this sort didn't require an answer. After all, you can hardly ask a fighter why he's fighting, can you? It would be like asking a man why he is a man.

The lingering silence saved him when Ustaz Ma'aruf suddenly raised his head and hastily shoved the small pen into his shirt pocket. There was a chill breeze coming from the mountain snow and bringing the frost with it. It swept through the land and it was as if it had extinguished the sounds of the bullets. Ustaz Ma'aruf got abruptly to his feet and Mansur did the same. They both looked towards the end of the lane. The three men took their boxes and disappeared from sight, but the air remained redolent with the smell of danger.

Picking up his box and positioning it on his shoulder, Ustaz Ma'aruf said: "Hey, the road looks safe."

Mansur bent down to pick up his box, but just as his hands grasped the edge, everything seemed to happen at once. A burning determination possessed him and began to ring in his forehead. This kind of thing had only happened to him two or three times before in his entire life: once when he was behind the plough in his father's field and heard the sound of metal breaking and saw the plough blade split into two pieces. Another time was when his white foal had died in his arms. He just couldn't shake off the significance of these events, as if some unknown power were kicking him, suddenly, in the nape of the neck. It was only an instant until he knew with absolute unshakable certainty that something dangerous was happening to him and that not all the power of earth and sky could help him lift the box.

Ustaz Ma'aruf hoisted his box up again and left Mansur standing in his place. Mansur, however, didn't move, but stayed where he was, watching Ustaz Ma'aruf as he approached the end of the lane. He stopped for awhile with all his senses alert to the utmost, just in case, as if he were about to leap into the air. He moved the box to his other shoulder, scraping the tiles with the sole of his shoe, ready for the decisive moment. Then he dashed all at once across the wide covered space behind the alley.

In the next instant there was a flood of bullets. Mansur could see the blazing pellets scraping the tiles of the courtyard alongside Ustaz Ma'aruf's feet. His heart began to beat wildly. Death trills were clamoring in his head while Ustaz Ma'aruf ran, leaping left and right in a crazily twisting line. He slid open the bolt on a door while the noisy whistling sound of bullets burst all around, above, in front and behind him. Thick and empty, the wind coming from the mountains began to howl in a miserable wounded voice.

There was a barrel filled with something standing in the middle of the courtyard. Between Mansur and Ustaz Ma'aruf were only a few steps, but they seemed a long endless expanse. Ustaz Ma'aruf was still holding his box on his shoulder where it protected his head from the bullets. The death trills still clamoured in Mansur's head like a chorus of sad captivating eyes. In front of a hole in the dirt another martyr fell. At the next instant Ustaz Ma'aruf had reached the barrel and was clinging to the ground directly behind it, like a nail suddenly pounded into it with a hammer. The bullets reached the spot with him, bursting noisily when they hit the barrel and leaving three holes in its middle from which water began to gush as if from the mouths of clay pitchers.

A cold silence settled once again, but the trills of death continued to fill Mansur's forehead. Ustaz Ma'aruf was crouched behind the barrel, trying with difficulty to turn around so that no part of him would be visible to the distant eyes observing him from atop the buildings in the Jewish quarter. He raised his head signalling thereby to Mansur that he had been able to grasp the situation. The barrel, whose water had begun to flow out of the three holes in it, would not serve as a shield for much more than a few minutes now. Once all the water was gone, Ustaz Ma'aruf would have to choose between two ways of dying: either he could run out from behind the barrel and be mowed down by the rifle shots just as the cats had been that morning, or he could wait another few minutes, behind the barrel until, when all the water had emptied out of it, the bullets could easily pass through its sides, and one of them hit him.

It was clear that the game pleased the marksmen, for a little while later there came still another bullet which punctured a fourth hole from which the water began to flow as well. Ustaz Ma'aruf spun around in confusion and the next minute a new bullet had hit the top of the barrel with a long warning whistle. On the other side of the courtyard three indistinct heads watched what was going on.

Mansur stepped to the edge of the lane and cautiously poked his head out. The tall building appeared between the low built houses like a citadel with its broad foundations. On the roof was an enclosure of sandbags that had been raised above the wall. He could see from where he was that there was a small empty square in the middle of the bags and it seemed to him that there was something black moving behind them. But then he thought he saw the cannon itself with its steel glittering in the light of the setting sun.

He made sure of the bullet in the firing chamber, then slowly and cautiously lifted the mouth of the gun to the corner of the wall, taking careful aim. His uncle had told him: 'Don't worry about the sights on the guns, just worry about your own nerves.' The empty square in the wall of sandbags appeared framed in the mouth of his gun when still more shots were fired. The holes in the barrel became one fiendishly large hole from which water flooded out. This, however, did not rattle Mansur's nerves and the next instant the hammer hit and an unbelievably wild thunder exploded. Then silence fell.

He loaded another bullet into the chamber and lay down on the wet pavement. In the middle of the courtyard, Ustaz Ma'aruf was once again getting ready to run. In the cold silence that had fallen there was not a sound except the water running from the holes in the barrel onto the pavement of the court-yard. Ustaz Ma'aruf, lifting his box to his shoulder and scraping the soles of his heavy black shoes, turned and made a dash for it. There was still one bullet that had not been fired. For those tense minutes there was nothing to be heard except the pound-ing of his feet on the pavement. On the other side of the court-yard where another lane began, three men cleared a way for him and he threw himself into it. Mansur stole another look at the wall of sand. It seemed quiet and ineffectual. In the next min-utes even the sound of running water trickled away. The holes were halfway up the barrel and the water had reached its limit. A high voice came from the edge of the courtyard: "You're a lion, you with the stick . . ."

This time, however, Mansur didn't get angry but began to laugh loud and heartily. The death trills inside his head faded away like bits of refuse.

—translated by Barbara Harlow

Abu al-Hassan
Ambushes an English Car

WHEN THE CAR DROPPED HIM OFF AT THE Nahaf crossroads, the man with the revolver switched off the motor and looked at him attentively. The emptiness was redolent with the sighing of the olive trees. Under them stood two men of the same family. One of them shook his head and pointed to the gun in Mansur's hands.

"Has that stick you've got there been much good?"

Unable to say anything, Mansur looked at him with the feeling that he was holding a dead piece of oiled wood in his hands. But the voice came once more: "Hope to see you again in Safad when there's no more fighting."

Still Mansur found nothing to say. As the engine started up again with a roar, the man released the brake and the car began to roll softly down the incline. It looked just the way Mansur had always imagined it: like a man without his pants on. When it had disappeared among the olive trees, Mansur took a deep breath and started up the road to Nahaf.

His uncle was out in the fields and so he put the gun in the kitchen where Umm al-Hassan was bending down over a mass of dough, kneading it with her brown hands plunged in up to the elbows. She looked up, biting her lips, when she saw Mansur watching her. Mansur placed his finger over his mouth asking her to be silent.

Quietly he left Nahaf crossing the stone walls which divided the olive fields and set out down the road to Majd al-Kurum where he arrived before lunch. When he was still some way off he could see his brother's car stopped in front of the door, lording over the middle of the road, but none of that disturbed him much.

At the door which was, as always, open, he untied his shoelaces, took off his shoes, and slipped inside. Walking past the door of the living room, he could see his father praying. Although his father had seen him too, Mansur hurried on to where his mother was standing in the courtyard of the clay house. He leaned over her hand and kissed it twice while his mother drew a deep breath and in turn kissed him on the forehead. For a moment she hugged him to her, but then released him, falling back a step and cautioning him in a hoarse whisper: "Your father's going to kill you . . . Where have you been?"

He answered in a steady voice which combined both hope and resolve: "Have mercy on me."

The next minute he heard a loud angry shout behind him: "Where have you been, you dog?"

Without turning around, Mansur responded with the simple truth: "In Safad."

"In Safad? What were you doing in Safad?"

"I took my uncle's gun and went to join the young men there. They're fighting."

"Who asked you to go and do that?"

"No one. I decided to do it myself."

His father shouted: "Turn around and talk to me face to face, you ingrate of a son."

Mansur turned around and looked at his father, directly into his angry eyes. His father came a step forward, and it was clear that he was going to have to use his hands. The next minute the blow which he had been expecting landed, but Mansur didn't move. When his mother moved to block the way between him and his father, he gently pushed her away from in front of him. Abu Qassim shouted again: "Say something."

Mansur licked his lips and felt a sweet warm taste.

Nonetheless he didn't raise his hand to his mouth to see whether or not it had begun to bleed, but went on looking his father straight in the eyes.

"If you're here and Qassim is in Haifa, one of us three had to go to Safad."

"Are you trying to sell me some kind of patriotism, you son of sin?"

Mansur licked his lips again and looked at his mother standing opposite them ready to throw herself between if Abu Qassim kept up the attack.

"I'm not trying to sell you patriotism. I just went to Safad."

Abu Qassim hesitated a moment. This was a new kind of battle, not the kind he was used to in years past. His son was looking at him angrily, when he presumably hit upon another point: "Did you return your uncle's gun?"

"Safe and sound."

"Why didn't you tell me?"

"You were in a hurry."

They waited another minute, like two cocks, but the anger was the kind that disappears, and now only the semblance of it remained.

"Your brother's in Haifa, running around with Jewish women. I've just dragged him out of there. He's an even more disobedient dog than you are, you wretch . . . and now you . . ."

At a loss, he stopped talking momentarily, measuring his son up and down with his eyes.

"Get out of my sight. Go to hell."

Smiling Mansur turned around and looked at his mother. After Abu Qassim had angrily slammed the living room door, his mother said in a subdued voice: "In any case, you have misbehaved."

"Where's the doctor?"

"At the coffeehouse. Ever since your father brought him back from Haifa, he's been going there every morning. He'll be back in an hour or so."

Even though the problem with his father had ended amicably enough, deep down inside him Mansur felt completely unplaced. He knew that he couldn't be satisfied with depending on his brother, the Doctor Qassim. Hanging around with

Jewish women! It was impossible for a woman ever to resist
Qassim. Doctor Qassim, who wanted to escape his peasantness
and become citified. Break the mold, as they say. Hanging
around with Jewish women. Jewish women. Wearing short
skirts and exposing their shoulders. He had seen them in al-
Carmel wearing short blue pants and walking shamelessly
about like that with a wrap no bigger than a folded handkerchief. The very land itself couldn't bear to look at them. Now
you don't have to . . . You're still ashamed of your brother
Qassim and you don't want to meet him. Instead of his being
ashamed of himself, you're being ashamed for him! Your big
brother. He crossed his hands in front of himself. Don't answer
and be careful not to raise your voice louder than his, even
though he's going about with Jewish women.

He thought for a minute about leaving the house again so
that he wouldn't have to meet Qassim face to face. He couldn't
for a minute imagine how his eyes would ever be able to look
upon that face of his.

In any case, however, he didn't meet Qassim that day, nor
that evening, nor even the next day. When his father finally sent
him to inquire about Qassim around noon, the owner of the
coffeehouse stretched his arm off towards the west, and said:
"He told me to tell you that he went back to Haifa."

*   *   *

When Abu al-Hassan returned to his home in Nahaf, the first
thing he saw was the old gun standing in the living room corner. He went over to it and picked it up as if it were something
very desirable, but in fact he didn't really desire it all that much.
He examined it carefully, turning it over in his hands at first,
then pulling out the broken firing pin and releasing the hammer, satisfied at the sound which it gave off. After that he examined the gun barrel and arm, tightening the fiber rope as if to
reassure himself that it still held firm. Only when he had finished all this did he smile contentedly to himself. He returned
the gun to its place and went off to the back courtyard where
Umm al-Hassan was doing the washing and stood watching her.

Even though she had aged before her time, her determination and strength of will had not changed, nor was her head-strongness any the less. She was one of those women who, because they can do whatever you might think of, one hardly ever finds sleeping or just sitting alone, catching their breath. Most of the time they make something for themselves to do even if you find a way to excuse them from work. Umm al-Hassan usually woke up before her husband, prepared breakfast, boiled the tea and then went outside to work on the little piece of land attached to the house. Then she would come back to straighten up and sweep the house and begin cooking lunch. She would do the washing and visit her neighbors, listening to what she didn't know and telling what she did. She would chase away the dogs, squeeze the tomato juice, feed the chickens, bring the eggs down to the store and buy what she needed for the day. If you saw her standing for a moment in the courtyard of the house, drying her hands on her colorful apron, you would know that she had just been thinking about something she had to do afterwards, and going back in those moments to devilish thoughts: like emptying the food into new dishes to give herself a chance to wash up the old dishes, or getting a dress out of the old trunk either to take in the seams or let them out or perhaps to mend some tears in it. Or else, if she couldn't find anything else to do, she would take refuge in the kitchen and start up again on her efforts to make harisa. For years now she hadn't been successful at this, and every time she made it Abu al-Hassan would take his first bite of the harisa and choke on it. He would scowl and not say anything, just look at her angrily with the piece of harisa still between his teeth. Then when he got up, she would greedily take a taste of it herself. Even so, she never admitted her failure until the following morning when she would get up and throw the rest of the harisa to the chickens. In spite of all these frustrated efforts of hers, she kept trying and always had such difficulty avoiding the job.

While she was busy hanging the laundry on the line, Abu al-Hassan said to her: "That boy should be hung by his ears and whipped . . . Did he tell you why he was late?"

"No, he didn't say."

"Anyway, the gun is still okay."

Umm al-Hassan wiped her hands on her apron and put

them on her hips: "How could you give the gun to a boy like Mansur? If he had died, it would have been your fault."

"When a man dies, there's no time to talk about the blame. Furthermore, he's not all that small."

She gave him a measured look from where she was standing. Sometimes when she looked at him reproachfully, he would think that she was about to leap at him and give him a good pounding. He always thanked God that so far in twenty years he hadn't given her an occasion for that.

"Listen, woman, I'm going now. If anyone asks about me, tell them that I've gone to Majd al-Kurum, or Acre, or to hell. Just make sure that you tell them I'm not here."

She bit her lower lip just as he expected her to do, and just as she always did when she wanted to avoid a question she didn't know how to answer. He didn't waste a minute before turning around and going back into the living room. Picking up his gun he went out the door without closing it after him. They were waiting for him behind the house and as soon as he arrived, they all walked off together in silence. With steps recognizable by their softness and without a moment's hesitation, they wandered off through the olive fields to the east. They knew practically every stone and every tree. And not only this, but they knew the history of every tree as well, who had been its previous owner and who owned it now, how much fruit it bore and how much it didn't, what its progress would be this season and what it had been last season. They went up behind the trees, far away from anything, avoiding any encounters with another person, until they came out behind Rameh where they turned off in an arc. Here they descended behind the rocks stretching to the crossroads.

As night began to fall, morosely and gloomily, a wall of fire rose up behind the hills and dampness spread, filled with the aroma of wet dirt. From their position it was easy for them to see where the road coming from Acre branched off into two roads. One of them went to the north to Sunhamata and the other climbed eastward to Faradiya and Safad. They chose a pile of rocks that had been heaped up and concealed themselves behind it, listening to the sounds. The four of them were almost the same age; they didn't know exactly, but it couldn't have been much more than forty. Only one of them looked like a really old man, and that was Abu al-Abd. For this reason Abu al-Hassan told him everything as it came to their attention: "Keep up your strength, Abu al-Abd," he would say, and Abu al-Abd would smile and shake his head without answering, as if the matter after all really didn't require an answer.

The old gun stood upright among them. Abu al-Hassan held it in his hands as if it were the fifth member of the party. The fibre cord hung limply from under the tip of its barrel. But it was warm and friendly and inspired a hidden confidence.

Abu al-Abd said: "Let's hope that we succeed before dark falls."

Abu al-Hassan thought that Abu al-Abd must really be an old man to imagine that the darkness could be any kind of frightening adversary. Oh, for those days when Abu al-Abd would be gone for a week at a time in the mountains, eating wood and thyme and not returning home until he had at least five English hats. What had happened to those days when a single person could go out walking from morning to night without so much as breathing hard? . . . That was twelve years ago, a long time, and the poor man was tired now and his will was gone. Oh, unfortunate Abu al-Abd, do you think that you can enter the battle now as you did in time gone by? Do you think that those who are fighting you now are the same English you fought twelve years ago? Do you think they've become old the way you have? Poor Abu al-Abd, if you only knew that they keep sending new generations and the old men go back to their homes. We're the only ones who grow old . . . As for them . . . A hidden rumbling came from the distance, like the growling of a cat. Abu al-Hassan dropped a bullet into the firing chamber and positioned the barrel of the gun on the edge of a rock, while the other three men got ready, silently tying up the lower ends of their long garments under their belts. The rumbling grew gradually louder while the glow behind the hills became cloudy. A funereal silence, about to explode, settled on the horizon.

"Be patient."

It was Abu al-Abd who said this, and in the silence his voice seemed hard and powerful, like in the old days. Meanwhile the rumbling grew still louder and after a few tautly strung moments a car appeared, approaching round the curve. It was moving slowly and there were two men sitting in the front seat. As Abu al-Hassan aimed at the driver he heard a hoarse whisper from his neighbor: "Have confidence, Abu al-Hassan. Get the driver."

The next instant he had squeezed the trigger and there was a thundering explosion. The car veered suddenly towards the edge of the road and rammed into the high stones. Even before Abu al-Hassan had loaded another bullet, the three men had leapt over the rocks and gone straight to the side of the car. They had done this so incredibly quickly that Abu al-Hassan himself had no time to decide what to do except to leap down and catch up with them. The driver had fallen back on the steering wheel and the other man in the car was quaking in fear. They dragged the driver by the collar out of the car and took away his revolver. All the while Abu al-Hassan kept the barrel of his gun pointing in his face. Knowing only one term of abuse in English, which was "fuckin," he kept repeating it monotonously over and over, in different tones, trying to find the right one, the way the English would say it themselves. But it was too hard.

Carefully and quickly they examined the car. Next to the driver there was a new English rifle as well as some cartridges. In front of the back seat was a long metal box. It was tightly closed and since there was no time to look into it, they took it with them. Abu al-Abd took over the attempt to persuade the soldier not to follow them. To do this, he used his hands and his eyebrows and broken Arabic. Finally when the soldier began to nod his head in agreement the others picked up the heavy box and started to run with it over the rough ground planted with olive trees. Meanwhile Abu al-Abd loaded his new gun and aimed it at the soldier, warning him to start back.

Ten minutes later or so, Abu al-Abd stopped and put his hand on Abu al-Hassan's shoulder. "Do you know what? We have to go back to that soldier and give him a good beating. We forgot to do that."

"What?"

"All my life, I've wanted to slap an English soldier in the face. And now I forgot to do it."

—translated by Barbara Harlow

The Child, His Father, and the Gun Go to the Citadel at Jaddin

MANSUR DIDN'T DARE GO BACK TO HIS UNCLE again. Instead he had heard that Abu al-Abd was hiding a brand new English rifle in his house. When he went there, however, his son Abdallah told him that his father had left the house and wouldn't be back for two days. Wasting no time then, Mansur climbed the hills to Tarshiha and arrived there before the sun had set. Hajj Abbas was sitting out on his small chair in front of the door rolling a cigarette out of rough dark tobacco. He had it all spread out on his lap, so he couldn't get up when he saw Mansur. He cut him off, laughing:

"So, you see I can't get up . . . How are you?"

Sitting down in front of him, Mansur replied: "Fine, and how are you, Uncle Hajj Abbas?"

Hajj Abbas looked at him with his sharp eagle-like eyes. His wrinkled face, burned by the sun, was severe. He was well-known in all the surrounding villages, but for all that, no one had formed any clear idea about him. There weren't two people who could agree on one opinion concerning Hajj Abbas: he was mean and profligate and ready to sell his pants for a few piastres, if his calculations showed that he stood to make a one piastre profit. At least that's what some people who knew him thought. But there were others who saw him as a clean, upright man who would give you the meat from his own neck if you were hungry.

Basically, however, Hajj Abbas dealt in tobacco and this may well have been the point which brought people to differ in their view of him. He was absolutely fair when it came to market prices and so his offers to the farmers were high or low according to whether the prices in Haifa were high or low. In the past Hajj Abbas had learned a lesson. This happened one day when the Qaraman Company had informed him that buying prices had dropped a great deal. Hajj Abbas had already made an arrangement with the farmers and had given his word. As a result his losses that year practically brought him to bankruptcy. From that day on, Hajj Abbas made his arrangements with the farmers on a different basis. They promised to give him the crop, but he himself made no promise on the price. The matter was left hanging ambiguously and he shipped the harvest to Haifa before paying for it. When the time came, there were, of course, problems about paying, but he was always able to end the differences to his own benefit.

Soon, however, matters became increasingly complicated and he found that if he wanted to continue successfully, he was going to have to get himself some kind of insurance. His first idea was to expand his operations. He fell back on giving credit and free loans. He was also able to reach an agreement with the Qaraman, Dik and Sulti Company whereby he would be given a monopoly on selling the crop from a given piece of land in Galilee which extended a distance of about five square kilometers around Tarshiha. Once all this was finished he breathed a deep sigh.

Hajj Abbas was generous in granting loans to anyone who needed it and no one knew him to have sent anyone in need away without responding to his request. He was not, however, particularly forbearing when it came to collecting on them, the precondition for the loan being in his view a friendly agreement. In order that the precondition be clear, however, it was written and recorded and he appended at the bottom the signatures of the witnesses.

Half the problems were solved by the court and the other half he solved himself. But however much quarrels might arise, Hajj Abbas was nonetheless eager to protect his personal connections with everyone. He visited them and kept in touch. No one was better than he at giving wedding presents. He gave his blessing on all the new births and his condolences when anyone died. He read the newspapers aloud to those who couldn't read, and would go to Acre to get the doctor if there were anyone sick who required it.

He had a taste for first-rate tobacco which he enjoyed down to the cigarette butt which he had made himself. When he wanted to really honor someone, he presented his guests with handfuls of the finest tobacco for them to take home with them.

He rolled his cigarette with precision, biting the edge of the paper and licking it with his tongue. Then he sealed it together and contemplated a moment the cigarette paper which was rolled carefully in the palm of his large hand. When he lit it he closed his eyes halfway in a special kind of pleasure, swallowing the smoke and then exhaling it in a thick cloud through his nose and mouth. Mansur watched him, thinking this might be a way to reach the heart of this man so capable of both desire and caution. It was as if he were all tied up in thorny threads. Hajj Abbas, however, as he usually did whenever he felt the situation required it, made the matter easy for him:

"It seems something's happening in Majd al-Kurum. Your father came by this morning and now here you are this evening. In any case I'm at your service. Your father told me that you were going to marry soon. You know that I'm ready to be of any service . . . If we don't celebrate with you young people, we old folks, what use are our lives?"

Hajj Abbas laughed as he usually did when talking with young people and old men. Deep down inside himself, he didn't believe that he was an old man. He had a kind of scorn for the young people of today, believing that if he got into a fight with any of them he had to be careful that he didn't break him into pieces like a dried tobacco plant. As for Mansur, however, no sooner had he collided with him than everything that had been in his head got changed around, until all he wanted now was to know the reason why his father had come to Hajj Abbas. He began to put his question, abruptly, as if it were an answer: "Did he want to borrow money?"

"Who?"

"My father."

"No. I myself thought at first that he wanted to borrow money. You know, I'm ready. Abu Qassim is very dear to me, but he didn't want money. He wanted to borrow the rifle."

"Your rifle?"

"That's right. You know, it's very precious to me. Even so, I gave it to him."

"For how much?"

Hajj Abbas laughed again and his throat gave out a childlike gurgling which then dwindled off. It pleased him that Mansur was being realistic and understood the way things really were and so he started enthusiastically to explain to him:

"We agreed on everything. He was the one who put down the conditions and I accepted them just as they were: he's paying a pound per day. Do you think that's such a lot? Well, it's not really. The rifle cost a hundred pounds. Anyway, he was satisfied and so was I."

"And if it gets lost or ruined?"

"Don't tell me your father has a hundred pounds to pay for it. But he could always pay the price in olives."

"Did you make him sign a paper."

"He's the one who wanted that. Distinguished men want the rights of the people. They don't accept oppression. I told him there was no place for papers between Hajj Abbas and Abu Qassim, but he insisted and I had no wish to make him angry."

He looked Mansur directly in the face while Mansur inhaled his cigarette with rare pleasure, trying to look natural and feeling that he couldn't. In the next minute, as he exhaled the smoke, he knew that Hajj Abbas had discovered the truth of his feelings. Hajj Abbas rested his elbows on his knees, saying in an excited voice:

"If I thought this was a mistake, you know, I would tear up the papers in front of you right now. But I didn't want to make the old man angry, so I let him do what he wanted to do. All I want is that he come back and bring my gun back."

"Where did he go?"

"I don't know, I don't know. I didn't ask him, and he didn't say."

He inhaled again and went back to leaning his back against the wall. He returned to the original subject: "Do you want to get married?"

"Of course."

"So, bridegroom, what is it that you want from me?"

Mansur glanced at him again in embarrassment, looking like a heap of flesh and misery on his small chair. Behind him the sun was setting, coloring the edges of the dark clouds in a blood-red hue. He looked upwards awhile. Throngs of black clouds were racing at each other. The next minute a heavy clap of thunder broke in the distance and Hajj Abbas said: "It's going to rain . . . what is it that you want?"

He stood up and looked at him from above.

"Nothing. I just came to ask about my father. I thought I might find him here with you and we'd go back to Majd al-Kurum together."

Hajj Abbas stood up and picked up his chair which looked smaller than it really was.

"It's going to rain. Why don't you sleep here tonight?"

"Thanks. I have something to do."

Without stopping he started to run across the stony hills while the clouds quietly poured forth rain like whispers. For the first time in his life he felt that his head was stuffed with clay, and that he was unable to work anything out. There were all these complications that he didn't believe: the rented rifle, why? And his father as well! What had brought him into the clutches of Hajj Abbas? This person was more like a worm. He didn't know his head from his tail. Didn't he know? Of course not! His father didn't meddle in this kind of thing. He was an old man and the only thing that mattered to him was the season just past and the season to come. But how?

He didn't slow down at all and his head was buzzing like a nest of hornets as he hurried down the narrow track which had been worn away by feet since the beginning of time. Nor could he contain his agitation as he entered the house. His mother, who was sleeping, woke up at the sound of his excited steps going about the house like a small gale. When she peeped out the door, she saw him standing directly in front of her, bigger than he had ever seemed before, angry, panting and drenched with rain.

"Where's my father?"

"He said there was a wedding in Acre."

Before saying anything he calmed down, even in spite of his surprise. His mother seemed to him such a poor woman, knowing nothing and needing nothing but a great love to last all her life. Does she really believe it's true that her husband has gone to Acre? And he had lied to her! What if he grabbed her now and shook her the way you shake a jar of milk, would she be able to see anything else? What was the hope?

He put on his long white shirt and got into bed, but his eyes didn't close all night. From the low window of the bedroom he watched the brilliant blood-red dawn. Soon the sun would disappear behind thick black clouds. Quietly he slipped from his bed and got dressed. He went out of the house, leaving the door wide open.

Shakib was in front of the coffeehouse smoking a cigarette. He was wearing long leather shoes and a khaki robe with large pockets and his short machine gun stood between his legs. When he saw Mansur coming he got up. Putting out his cigarette he picked up his machine gun by its middle, like someone long used to carrying such a gun, and asked: "Where's your weapon?"

"I didn't find anything. All the doors were locked."

"So why did you come then?"

"I don't know. I'll take my orders there."

He measured him up and down with his steady black eyes, then stepped in front of him without a word. Shakib was an enigmatic man, rigid as a basalt wall. He knew every family in Majd al-Kurum and the neighboring villages, but they in turn did not know him. Shakib was always able to procure weapons, and yet no one knew where he got them, so that most days when the English arbitrarily searched for arms Shakib managed to guard a revolver, or a rifle, or a machine gun. One day, five years ago, Majd al-Kurum saw him carrying a huge machine gun. It was a Vickers model. Because it was difficult to conceal, he had dismantled it, and buried the small pieces outside in the village. Five years later when he went back to get it, it was all corroded and impossible for him to reassemble, so he sold it as scrap metal.

The English arrested him immediately whenever one of their soldiers was reported killed anywhere around Galilee. As a result, he had come to know every Palestinian jail and most of the officers in the British army. Madly passionate for weapons, he was nonetheless ready to strangle an English officer with his bare hands if ever given half a chance. For a long time he was called a scoundrel, even though he wasn't really like that, but rather polite and diffident and acknowledging the service to others as an obligation. When he married, the families of Majd al-Kurum saw him as an ideal husband eager to protect and provide a worthy life for his wife and child. For days on end he would disappear without anyone knowing where he was hiding. Then, when he returned, Majd al-Kurum would hear the mysterious news of dangerous things happening in one place or another around Galilee. Everyone was, however, sworn to silence.

Shakib didn't talk much to anyone about his own life, but every man in Majd al-Kurum knew that he received all his clothes, right down to the underwear, from the English army camps and that somewhere in his house he had uniforms of English officers of different ranks. Once while he was ploughing in his field outside Majd al-Kurum he had even had the opportunity to wear the uniform of an English major.

His marksmanship was unbelievably good and he was able to use a wide variety of weapons with skill and confidence. He was well-known as well for his beautiful voice and he used to sing on occasion at the weddings in Majd al-Kurum of deep affliction and the sadness of love and land and sky.

His steps were broad and heavy as he took the shortcut across the rugged terrain. Mansur followed with difficulty without understanding whether he was welcome. Before the morning was over the two of them had crossed the hills of Jaddin. From the heights surrounding it they saw the mighty citadel standing atop the plain and encircled by wood huts inside a girth of thick barbed wire.

Shakib sat down, spreading his legs as if they were two big pieces of firewood and pointing with the muzzle of the rifle toward the citadel. He appeared calm, relaxed and unbothered by anything exactly as he had appeared that morning sitting in the square of Majd al-Kurum. He spoke to Mansur in his sad, quiet voice which seemed as free as did the man himself: "I don't understand much about history, but this citadel is really old. Anyway we're not here to study it, we're here to occupy it."

Once more he looked at Mansur, as if he hadn't seen him before. He smiled: "Even though you're not carrying a weapon! . . . But don't worry too much, now when the men are gathered, we'll see. Probably some of them will discover at the last minute that they're sick and can't use their weapons."

For a while Mansur gazed at the citadel. To him it seemed forbidding and closed, like a mountain with no caves, and the idea of occupying it struck him as a joke.

"We're the only ones in this area. All the men are approaching from Tarshiha, Yaraka, and al-Kabri. Maybe al-Shishakli will bring some of his men as well . . . But that's not the important thing. The important thing is that this citadel is filled with arms. If it were easy for you to enter it, then you would worry about all you had to carry with you . . . this way your coming isn't in vain. You can devote yourself to praying during the fight. If the heavens answer your prayers, you'll get a weapon."

He smiled briefly to himself, then got up and started down the slope on his hard steady feet. The men were waiting halfway between Jaddin and Umqa. There were two mortar guns in front. The rifles looked old, but they were sound. When the two of them arrived, the first thing Mansur saw was his father's face.

He was sitting on the ground at the far end of the circle with his hands resting on the gun, Hajj Abbas's gun no doubt, and listening to the remarks of a man with a beard wearing a belt filled with bullets. He was in the middle of explaining the details. He used his hands and gave a brief outline.

He had expected that, he was deeply convinced of it. But even so, he continued in a way to repress the lie to himself because he hadn't wanted it, and yet had been certain that he would find his father sitting there, waiting for the battle. For agonizing hours he had clung to the tiny hope of not finding him there. What happened next was simple: his father raised his eyes from the ground and saw him standing at the other side of the circle next to Shakib. His face, however, remained frozen as if he were looking at some man he didn't know. Once the man with the beard had finished his explanation, Abu Qassim stood up and went over to his son. He stood next to him without looking at him. Only when the march began did he speak to him in a whisper: "You shouldn't have come. It's not right to leave your mother alone."

"That's what I wanted to tell you. Why don't you give me your gun and go back to Majd al-Kurum?"

Abu Qassim shoved the gun in front of his son's face. It seemed to sparkle in the morning light as if it had just come from the factory.

"It's not my gun. It belongs to Hajj Abbas. I put down the rental price for it and gave my olives as security, so I'm not going to surrender it to anyone, into any hands but these."

Mansur waited a little and then asked in a peremptory voice: "Why did you join the attack on Jaddin?"

"The revolution has begun. That's the whole thing."

"No, that's not it. You wanted to get a rifle from Jaddin, to give me on my wedding night, just like you promised me."

Abu Qassim didn't answer, but pressed his lips together and took a few steps, so that he suddenly saw the men who were in the front. Looking around him he saw Shakib humming a tune to himself. He grabbed him with his hands and could feel the strength of his arm and its hardness.

"Listen, Mansur. This generation is an accursed generation. You have to know that from the beginning. Their heads are like stones, so don't waste your time trying to satisfy them. You can't

fool them. Your father and my father and all this accursed generation, you can only work with them by cleverness. Now do
you know what you have to do? Just try to protect him."

"Do you really think we can occupy the citadel?"

"No, I don't really think so, but the attack will be useful,
and who knows, a miracle might happen."

There were low wooden houses surrounding the citadel on
all sides and around these he saw thick barbed wire. A group of
men had gathered on the road to cut off the help that might
arrive from Nahariya. Meanwhile the men on the slope settled
down to wait.

Some distance away Mansur saw Shakib crawling towards
the wire. He had seen where it was attached by rope and was
about to shake it from afar so that the mines which had been set
there would explode. Before Shakib reached the wire, however,
bullets poured forth. For the next few minutes, the hill was
alight with sparks. Mansur couldn't catch up with his father,
but all the men were moving rapidly from one place to another.
He couldn't see anything more than their kaffiyas fluttering like
small white flags among the stones and thorn trees. The bullets
rained down around Shakib making it impossible for him to
move except to wait completely crouched down with his arms
on a bundle of rope and a roof of uninterrupted firing above
him. It occurred then to Mansur that the situation might well
go on like this indefinitely, that the two sides would go on firing
bullets and mortars of steel and stone without knowing anything about each other. If he only knew the natural layout of
Jaddin, couldn't he imagine some other way? Then when the
mortar shells began to blow up the wooden houses one by one,
the sound of the bullets died down. Shakib moved a step and
began to creep forward like a short viper while the mortars
exploded here and there silencing the guns behind the others.
By the time Shakib reached the barbed wire, the sound of the
bullets coming from the wood huts had ceased. This made it
easy for him to tie carefully the ropes and slip nimbly away. In
the next instant the wire began to shake violently pulling out
the ropes while the mines exploded all at once producing a
dreadful noise and hurling a storm of sand and stones to a

tremendous height. Then suddenly the sound of rifles and machine guns and mortar shells fell silent, as if waiting.

When the smoke cleared, the wood huts reappeared, impotent, crippled and wholly exposed in front of the men lying in ambush on the hill. Mansur slipped from behind and caught up with the front line. After some long minutes of expectant silence the men began to advance, slowly, cautiously at first. Then one man, and another, stood up and both started to run, carrying their guns over their heads, towards the abandoned huts. It was as if they were declaring that a new stage of the assault had begun. The men left their hiding places and started slipping over the hill, releasing as they went a huge roar. Only when they had reached the shredded barbed wire did fire from the windows of the mighty fortress get to them, and they fell to the ground once again.

For an hour it was impossible to advance a single step. The firing was profuse and uninterrupted and it wasn't easy to tell exactly where it was coming from. Mortar shells began again to fall around the tenacious fortress, then it was silent. Mansur said to himself: "If only they'd run out of mortar material." He was still clinging to the rock where Shakib, looking dusty and tired and shattered, had crawled. He sat down next to him, hugging his machine gun and shaking his head.

"Do you understand? I didn't fire a single bullet. How are we shooting?"

He looked at his machine gun as if to blame it, then he gave Mansur a push with his elbow.

"Here we are. Everything's finished. The British will come and surround us."

Dismayed, Mansur asked: "What happened?"

"Nothing, of course . . . It was easy to demolish the wooden houses and half the barbed wire. They probably knew this and so they dug deep trenches between the houses and the citadel. When the mortar shelling began, the retreat began. They were watching us from the citadel. We didn't do anything. The citadel can hold out for two days, but does that guarantee that the British won't come?"

"But if we could destroy . . ."

"Everything's finished. Here we are. It was a Bedouin attack and couldn't tell its head from its tail. But we'll learn."

"What about my father?"

"Let him take care of his own affairs himself. It's not your job to tell him what he has to do."

The sound of the bullets began to wane and only a few stubborn shots gave notice of their existence from time to time. Mansur turned around and started to climb up the hill next to Shakib. In the meantime the men were retreating one by one and firing off what remained of their ammunition. When Mansur reached the road he sat down to wait while Shakib continued on his way. They didn't exchange a single word of farewell. He felt a repeated pain in his throat and couldn't get rid of the sensation which had been troubling him since the morning that he had forgotten something. After all, it was really ridiculous to go into battle without weapons, as if you were going to a wedding. Even a wedding requires that a man go armed. Any kind of combat, and wasn't this combat? Fighting each other with stones in your hands. Struggling, banging your bare head against a wall. Wasn't it a disgrace to go on like this without arms? Men got their weapons by force, not by asking permission and not by going sometimes to Nahaf and sometimes to Kisra to borrow a gun.

To own a gun for one courageous moment, maybe with a bayonet on it as well. But whoever said that the sky rained rifles the way it rained manna and quails? For the last ten years Shakib had been able to steal hundreds, at least, of weapons. He didn't ask permission from anyone. What are you waiting around for, Mr. Mansur? Do you think you're going to find a rifle or a machine gun on the doorstep of your house some morning? This is the revolution! That's what everyone says, and you're not going to know what that means until you sling a gun over your shoulder, a gun that shoots. How long are you going to wait?

The skies filled suddenly with the sound of thunder and men's voices rose from the top of the hill. Between the thick clouds an airplane was visible glittering like a long silver platter. The plane made two wide circles over the hill and the citadel and then circled high once more. Before he saw it again bombs began to go off on the hilltop like a cordon of black trees. To the north armored cars appeared haughtily from over the al-Kabri road and opened fire on the hill. The voice of a frightened man shouted from the bottom of the valley: "Here come the English boys!"

The white kaffiyas fluttered about looking for a hiding place. The sun was veiled behind the dark black clouds and the skies began to rain lightly. For just awhile the men were confused, then they began to climb the hill turning toward the south. It was clear that the Nahariya-al-Kabri road to the north was being patrolled by the English armored cars that had come to assist Jaddin, and so the only open road was to the south. Whatever you decided to do, the narrow road climbed straight up. The rifles opened fire on the raised roofs of the hill across the valley.

The armored cars were practically breathing on the Jaddin citadel and from their windows they kept up a heavy fire. Meanwhile the first rows of men were passing Mansur on their way towards the south. Although Mansur was waiting, out of breath, for his father to arrive, he nonetheless couldn't rely on this weak, trembling expectation and so he began to go on down, stubbornly but cautiously. When he reached the edge of the firing the bearded man who was carrying his machine gun aimed and stopped him. He was swathed with belts of cartridges and all muddy. His face was streaked with black. Grabbing Mansur by the hand, he shoved him roughly backwards, shouting: "Where do you think you're going? Are you crazy?"

Mansur shook his hand greedily and before the man had recovered from the impact of the gesture Mansur had grabbed the arm of the rifle with both hands and tugged it violently to himself: "If you're afraid, give me your gun . . . My father's still there."

The man, however, held on to his gun. Quietly, with a quick movement which Mansur could neither see nor follow, he stood up, snatching his gun with him and causing Mansur to lose his balance. His voice came from his chest and his scowling face

streaked with black smiled savagely: "Let's look for him together. He's from Majd al-Kurum isn't he?"

Mansur nodded his head in assent while the man picked up
his gun and moved forward, placing his large feet hard and
judiciously in the muddy puddles and skillfully concealing himself behind the piles of stones. The bombs had begun to go off
behind the two of them as they beat their retreat step by step. At
the sound of a violent thunder, the man looked at Mansur. It
was hard to tell much from his appearance, stained as it was
with mud and smoke.

"He must be a tough old man. Our front lines were here.
Does this mean he went beyond them? . . . Are you sure he did-
n't retreat?"

"Of course."

As he said this, Mansur's heart began to beat violently, like a
rooster being slaughtered, and he felt a violent danger all
around him. He swallowed his saliva with difficulty and ended
up staring at the ground. "No, no, he didn't retreat. I was at the
head of the road . . . if he had retreated, he would have had to
pass by me."

The man wiped his forehead with his sleeve and asked: "Do
you want to go further ahead?"

"Yes."

The man thought awhile and picked up his gun.

"Try to shield me. I'll go on by myself and come back to you
here . . . Don't move a single step."

The steel of the rifle was wet and he felt a tremor run
through his hand when he seized it. He began ever more vora-
ciously to look around him at everything washed in rain water.
The sound of the many bullets had lost its meaning now and
become a part of the thunder and lightning and dark clouds
which stretched like a low roof of darkness above his head. He
pressed the machine gun to his chest, tightly closing his eyes for
just a second, then he went back to examining the muzzle in
front of him, bending his fingers around the hammer and taking sight with his narrowed eyes at the rocks and the thorn trees
lavishly bathed in rain water.

Time passed cold and heavy as he dragged his steps through

the deep pools of mud, as if shackled and tied to the mountain. He was angry but exhausted as well. His teeth were chattering and the pounding had started again in his chest. He trembled like a steel spring from mud and fright.

Mansur was filled with expectation. It throbbed inside him to a point where it seemed that whatever it was that he was expecting must inevitably happen. It couldn't escape him. When he saw the man with the beard in the distance, a stooped, coarse spectre, carrying another shadowy-like figure on his shoulders, he took in the sight calmly, as if he had seen it hours and hours before and was ready for it.

He stayed where he was, and knelt down on one knee, washing himself in the rain and staring at his father being carried on the man's shoulders. When they had drawn close to him he saw that his father's hand was closed carefully around the middle of the gun and that he had wrapped the strap around his forearm. Both men were covered with blood which had soaked through their clothes like the last protection from the rain. When they were right near him, the bearded man said:

"Here. I'll get a mule when we reach the road. From there, you take your father straight to Majd al-Kurum. Walk behind me and keep your eye on the road at the back of us. They've left the citadel and intend to meet up with us. At least that's what I'm thinking."

Mansur didn't utter a single syllable, but walked quietly behind the man. Meanwhile the clouds had broken and sunbeams were streaming forth checkering the small stretch of land behind them. The hill looked deserted and forlorn. The cannon had stopped firing, but the sound of gunshots continued to rain down heedlessly from different directions. When they reached the road, the man lowered Abu Qassim from his shoulders, propping his back against a thick tree trunk. One of the old man's hands clutched his stomach while the other held on stubbornly to the rifle. Mansur handed the machine gun to the man, saying in a hoarse voice: "I don't want to see him . . . Tell me, is the wound serious?"

"The bullet seems to be in the intestines. If he doesn't bleed to death on the road, a doctor can save him . . . Do you know a doctor? Anyway I'm going to go now and get a donkey. You'd better get to Majd al-Kurum quickly . . . I asked you, do you know a doctor?"

Mansur looked at his father crumpled at the foot of the tree trunk. Blood was gushing from between the fingers of his muddy hand which was pressed over his stomach. His eyes were closed and his other hand, clenched around the rifle, looked wooden and dead.

"Do you know a doctor?"

"A doctor? My brother Qassim is a doctor. Qassim. Of course . . . But he . . ."

"What are you waiting for then? I'm going to get a donkey for the old man."

The moans began to lessen and then to increase again. The sun by now had completely set and all sounds had died away. In the utter silence the moans had a grievous effect, together with the blood pouring from between the convulsive fingers so that you could almost hear it. Mansur stood in the wet emptiness watching his father slowly dying, impotent and unmoving except for the deep throbbing which shook him. His veins were like taut wires bulging from his hands and extending around the torso of the rifle. Finally they all began to blur together: the tree, the man and the rifle, from behind the darkness of the angry rain, and through his tears. But to Mansur, they were not together. There was only the quiet corpse.

—translated by Barbara Harlow

The Child
Goes to the Camp

I T WAS WAR-TIME. NOT WAR REALLY, BUT HOSTILITIES, to be precise . . . a continued struggle with the enemy. In war the winds of peace gather the combatants to repose, truce, tranquility, the holiday of retreat. But this is not so with hostilities that are always never more than a gunshot away, where you are always walking miraculously between the shots. That's what it was, just as I was telling you, a time of hostilities.

I lived with seven brothers, all of them strong. Father didn't much care for his wife, but this may have been because she had borne him eight children during a time of hostilities. Then there was our aunt and her husband and five children who also lived with us. And our old grandfather. Whenever he found five piastres on the table or in the pocket of one of the many pairs of pants which would be hanging up, he went straight out and bought a newspaper. As you know, he couldn't read, so in order to find out what was being done, he had to have one of us read aloud to him the latest bad news.

At that time—but first let me tell you that it wasn't a time of hostilities in the sense that you might think. That is, there wasn't really a war. In fact there was no war at all. The whole thing is that we were eighteen people from different generations living in one house, which would have been more than enough at any time. None of us had managed to find work, and hunger—which you may have heard of—was our daily worry. That is what I call the time of hostilities. You know, there is absolutely no difference. We fought for our food and then fought each other over how it would be distributed amongst us. Then we fought again. Whenever there was a moment of silence, my grandfather would carefully get his rolled-up newspaper out from under his clothes and look at everyone with his small alert eyes. This meant that five piastres had been pilfered from some pocket—if there had been five piastres—or from somewhere. A quarrel would follow. My grandfather kept hold of the newspaper, resisting the voices with the silence of an old man who has lived long enough to have heard all sorts of clamor and quarrels without seeing in them any reason for answering or concern. Then, when the noise had quieted down, he would lean towards the nearest child (he didn't, however, trust the girls) and give him the newspaper, always keeping hold of it by the edge, so no one would take it from him.

Isam and I were ten years old. He was a little bigger than I was, and still is, and he considered himself the leader of his brothers, my cousins, just as I consider myself the leader of my brothers. After long efforts, my father and my aunt's husband finally found a daily task for us. Together we were to carry a big basket and walk for about an hour and a quarter until we came to the vegetable market sometime in the afternoon. You don't know what the vegetable market was like: the shops were beginning to close their doors and the last of the trucks loaded with what was left from the day were getting ready to leave the crowded street. Our job—mine and Isam's—was easy and difficult at the same time. We had to find stuff to fill our basket. From in front of the shops or behind the cars. Even from the tops of tables if the owner happened to be taking a nap or was inside his store.

I tell you it was a time of hostilities. You don't know how a fighter runs between shots all day long. Isam would shoot off like an arrow just in order to snatch a torn head of lettuce or a bunch of onions or maybe even some apples from between the wheels of a truck which was about to move. My role was to hold off the fiends—the rest of the children. If they tried to get hold of an orange, I would see it in the mud before them. We worked all afternoon, Isam and I, struggling with the other children, or the shop owners or the truck drivers, sometimes even with the police. The rest of the time I fought with Isam.

That was the time of hostilities. I tell you this because you don't know. The world at that time had turned upside down. No one expected any virtue. This would have seemed too ridiculous. This itself was virtue's triumph. Fine. When a man dies, so too does virtue. No? Well then, let's suppose that, in a time of hostilities, it was your job to safeguard the first and foremost virtue, which is to keep yourself alive. Everything else is secondary. But in a time of continuous hostilities, nothing is secondary. Everything comes first.

Once the basket was filled, it was up to us to carry it back home. This was to be everybody's meal on the following day . . . But of course Isam and I had agreed between ourselves that we would eat the best of whatever was in the basket on the way home. There was never any objection to this agreement from either of us, and we never gave it away. It just happened. We were together in a time of hostilities.

Winter was very hard that ill-fated year and we were carrying a very heavy basket (I haven't forgotten this, it was like falling into a trench during a battle, a trench that held you like a bed). I ate the apples and we left through the market gate and went on out into the main street. We spent nearly ten minutes in the middle of people, cars, buses, and shop fronts without exchanging a word (the basket was really heavy and both of us were completely absorbed in eating), when suddenly . . .

But no, I can't describe it. It's absolutely indescribable. It's as if the enemy had you at swordpoint, and you had no weapon of your own, and then just at that instant you find yourself in your mother's arms . . .

Let me tell you what happened. Isam and I were carrying the basket, just as I said, and there was a policeman standing in the middle of the road. The street was wet and we had no shoes. Perhaps it was because I was looking at the policeman's thick heavy shoes, but anyway, suddenly I saw it there under his shoes. It was about six meters away, but I knew, maybe from the color, that it was more than one pound.

In situations like this, we don't stop and think. People talk about instinct. That's fine. I don't know if the color of paper money has anything to do with instinct, but it does have a connection with that kind of savage force, crime, the power to strangle someone in a moment, which is there deep inside every one of us. What I do know is that a man, in a time of hostilities, doesn't think when he sees a paper bill under a policeman's shoes, even if he's six meters away and carrying a basket of rotten vegetables. And that's what I did. I threw away what was left of the apple and dropped the basket. Probably Isam staggered under the sudden weight of the basket which I left in his hands, although he too had seen the money only a second after I did. But of course I had already pounced, compelled by this unknown force which drives the rhinoceros to attack blindly. I wanted it more than anything. I bumped up against the policeman's legs with my shoulder so that he fell back in alarm. I lost my balance, but I didn't fall and at that instant—just when the foolish think that it's all over—I saw it. Five pounds. All I had to do was pick it up as I fell. But I got up faster than I fell and I ran faster than I got up. Practically the whole world began to run after me. There was the policeman's whistle and the sound of his shoes pounding on the stones of the street right behind me. Isam screamed. The buses rang their bells. People were shouting . . . were they really right behind me? You can't say and neither can I. But I ran until I was sure that no one in all the armored squadrons could ever catch me. With the savvy of a ten-year-old child, I took another road. Maybe it was because I thought that Isam would point the policeman in my direction. I don't know. I didn't turn around, I just ran, and didn't even think how tired I was. I was a soldier, fleeing the scene of the battle I had been forced to enter. There was nothing in front of me but to keep running and the world with its shoes was behind me at my heels.

I didn't reach home until after dark and when the door was opened for me I saw just what I had been expecting, deep inside me, to see. Seventeen people waiting in the house for me. They studied me quickly but carefully and I met their glare from the doorway where I stood. My hand closed around the five pounds in my pocket and my feet remained firm on the ground.

Isam was standing between his mother and father. He was furious. Most likely there had been a quarrel between the two families before my arrival. I looked in appeal to my grandfather who was sitting in the corner wrapped up in his neat brown aba and staring at me in amazement. A wise man, a real man, knows how he's supposed to see the world. The only thing he wanted from the five pounds was a really big newspaper that day.

I waited impatiently for the argument. Isam, of course, had lied and told them that he was the one who found the five pounds and that I forced it from him. Not only that, but that I had made him carry the heavy basket by himself the whole way. Didn't I tell you that it was a time of hostilities? None of us bothered about Isam's protest, about whether he was telling the truth or lying. That was something that couldn't matter less. Isam maybe wasn't lying, but it was certain that no one worried about the truth. Furthermore, here he was, content to humble himself and even admit for the first time that I had hit him and that I was stronger than he was. But what did all of this matter, given the really important questions?

His father was thinking of something completely different. He was ready to accept half the money and my father wanted the other half. If I succeeded in keeping the whole amount, which was my right, I would have it all, but if I gave up this right, then I lost everything and they would split the money.

They didn't really know what it meant for a child to have five pounds in his pocket in a time of hostilities . . . I threatened them all, using words I had never in my life used, to leave home forever. The five pounds were for me and only me.

Of course, you must know. They were absolutely furious and lost all control. Everybody was against me. First of all, they just warned me. But I was prepared for even more than that, so they began to hit me. Of course, I couldn't defend myself, and since I was trying as best as I could to protect my pocket with the five pounds in it, it was especially hard for me to ward off their well-aimed blows. In the beginning my grandfather watched the battle excitedly, but then, when it began to lose its interest, he got up and stood in front of them and whispered to me to hold on to him. He proposed a settlement. He said that the grown-ups had no right to the money, but that on the first sunny day I had to take all the children in the house to some place where we could all spend the money in any way we wanted.

I was just about to refuse the proposal when I was struck by something I saw in my grandfather's eyes. I didn't exactly understand what it was, I only felt that he was lying and that he wanted me to keep quiet.

You know that a child of ten—in a time of hostilities—can't understand things (even if there is any need to understand them) the way an old man like my grandfather can. But that's what happened anyway. He wanted his newspaper every day for a whole week and he was trying to appease me whatever the price.

So we came to an agreement that evening, but I knew that it wouldn't end there. I would have to guard the five pounds every instant, night and day. And I had to put off the other children. I also had to resist all my mother's attempts to bribe me which she could never refrain from. She told me that evening that five pounds would buy two rotls of meat, or a new shirt for me. Or medicine if it were needed. Or books, since they were thinking of sending me to school next summer. But what was the use of all this talk? It was as though she wanted me to stop and clean my shoes while running between gunshots.

I didn't know exactly what I was going to do. But all the next week I managed to hold the other children off with a thousand lies, which, or course, they knew were lies, but they never said anything about it. There was no virtue here. You know. It was a different question and revolved around only one kind of virtue: five pounds.

My grandfather, however, understood matters and he wanted his newspaper at a fair price for his role in the whole story. When a week had gone by, he began to grumble. He knew (he had to know it since the truth doesn't escape an old man like him) that I wasn't going to buy him his newspaper. He felt that he had lost his opportunity, but he didn't do anything to recover it.

By the time another ten days had gone by, everyone believed that I had spent the five pounds and that the hand I kept in my pocket was holding on to nothing, that it was all a trick. But my grandfather knew that the five pounds was still in my pocket, and that night in fact he got up and tried to take it while I was sleeping (I always slept with my clothes on). I woke up, however, and he went back to his bed and to sleep without a word.

I told you, it was a time of hostilities. My grandfather was sad because he didn't get his newspaper, not because I broke a promise which had not been agreed to. He understood the time of hostilities, and so for the next two years he didn't scold me for whatever I did. In the meantime Isam forgot the story too. Deep inside him—like an unruly child—he understood exactly what had happened. We continued our daily trips to the vegetable market. We argued less than at any other time before and we spoke little. It seemed that something—a strange wall suddenly went up within him—it was still a time of hostilities—I was the one who breathed a sigh of relief—I don't know how—it seemed that something else was in the air.

I remember that I kept the five pounds in my pocket for five weeks. I was looking for the right moment, when the time of hostilities would be over. But whenever this was about to happen, it seemed as if we were getting deeper into hostilities rather than out of them.

How can you possibly understand that? I had the five pounds, but something kept me from using it. As long as it was in my pocket it seemed to me like a key that I held in the palm of my hand and that I could use at any time to open the door and walk out. But whenever I got close to the lock I smelled still another time of hostilities behind the door, further away, like going back once more to the beginning.

What followed is not important. I went one day with Isam to the market. While I was trying to grab a bunch of chard which was in front of the wheels of a truck, the truck slowly started to move. At the last minute I slipped and fell underneath it. It was really lucky that the wheels didn't go over my legs, but stopped just as they hit them. In any case, I regained consciousness in the hospital. The first thing I did—as you must have guessed—was to look for the five pounds. But it wasn't there.

I think it was Isam who took it when he was with me in the car on the way to the hospital. But he didn't say and I didn't ask. We just looked at each other and understood. I wasn't angry because it had been fun and I had shed my blood to take the five pounds. I was only sad that I had lost it.

You won't understand. It was in a time of hostilities.

—translated by Barbara Harlow

The Child Discovers that the Key Looks Like an Axe

I T REALLY DOES LOOK JUST LIKE A SMALL AXE, AND IF the back of it were not topped off with a ring you would really think that it was a miniature kind of axe. I don't remember now who it was who had made it, or whether it was designed for that purpose, but at times it even came to seem so familiar and habitual that the image of the axe would disappear and nothing would remain except the key.

In the beginning I thought that I was the only one who saw the shape of a small axe in it. At that time I used to see a lot of things differently from what they really were, and to myself I thought that maybe I was suffering from some dangerous sickness which made things look different to me than they did to others. Two or three times I had been unable to convince my brother that the clouds which were visible to both of us, were practically a lion. He would just say: They're only clouds; and I could never convince him that the clouds would soon break up and become something else.

In any case this is not what happened with the key. In fact I didn't tell anyone that it looked like a small axe. Then one day it happened that I learned quite by surprise that this fact was much more widely known than I had realized. When I complained to my father that I still couldn't chop the firewood with him because the axe was too heavy, he stood there and looked at me in wonder. Then he took the key out of his belt and said to me laughingly: "Perhaps you need an axe like this?" I looked at the key in surprise and almost started to smile, but my father scolded me with an insult which was somewhere between anger and resignation: "The devil take you!"

It was a bulky key, dark reddish-brown, except that its head was shiny and took the shape of an axe blade, broad at the end and narrow at the head which was connected to the handle. My father himself didn't know who had made it and said that when he was a child he had seen it with his father. He said that his father too had seen it as if it were a small axe which could be transformed into a key.

Undoubtedly the shape of the key sometimes produced a kind of scorn on the part of those who were seeing it for the first time. We would be there in the house, expecting the guest, when he saw the key, to say to us: what a strange thing; then they would almost always say: "Is this your axe?" My father would answer coldly, telling him in turn about his father: "No, this is our key. Our axe is in the barn. Would you like to see it?" Every time we children would laugh and laugh, just as if we had never heard this answer before. That always pleased my father a great deal.

As far as we were concerned the key had a whole collection of virtues which entered slowly but surely into our life. For one thing it was the only key which time had not been able to destroy. Every man, woman and child in the village knew that this little key was the key to the Jabr house. But the people in the neighboring villages knew this too, and so if it ever got lost or dropped, it would be returned to the house, just like that, as if by itself. The key was also used for many other things because its edge was very sharp. Also its heavy back could be used as a small hammer. I remember that my mother told one of her relatives that her mother-in-law had used the edge of it one day to peel onions when she had lost her knife and that her uncle for days could smell the odor of onions all around him without knowing where it was coming from.

*   *   *

I think I must have forgotten about the key when I went to study in Jerusalem and was away from all the things of the village, the absence of a youth who has begun to discover a new world. But the world which I afterwards discovered was the same world which I had left behind. How should I explain what happened to me? It seems every bit as complicated as it is simple . . . I lived in Jerusalem for three years straight. I saw my father on a number of occasions, but these were brief. He would come to Jerusalem and sit in my tiny room and I would see the key in his belt. It was only at those times that the village and everything about it would come into my head like a mysterious fragrance. But then afterwards the key would disappear when my father disappeared. I think I began to discover a world without keys, a new exciting world without limits. That, however, as I realized later, was only a delusion. One day when I came home from the college the landlady told me that a man named Yahya had been asking about me and that he would return that evening. When I asked her where he came from, she told me that he came from the village. Then I remembered who Yahya was: he was a skinny young man, very brown, and well-known among us for his silence. Nonetheless under that silence he concealed unlimited maliciousness and my mother used to say that he was a "serpent in the straw". What had brought him to Jerusalem just now?

"He said that he had come about some key affair."

"Key?"

The whole world suddenly stopped in front of me. Maybe because it was the first time in my life that I heard the word key without the definite article. It has always been "the key." What was it now that made it simply "key"? It all seemed to be very complicated to me, even to be announcing some kind of disaster. I waited for Yahya to come that evening. He greeted me coldly and when he sat down, I began looking at him suspiciously. After a little while his voice began to lose that coldness with which bearers of bad news arm themselves.

"Your life is before you."

"Who?"

"Your father."

Gently he removed the key from his belt and placed it in the middle of the whirlpool which was raging in my head, as if by driving it into place he could stop this horrible spinning. He stood up.

"He died honorably and courageously, just as he lived. If it weren't for him, they would have occupied . . ."

He fell silent, leaving me to fill in the rest of the picture of a man whom I would never again be able to see, ever. He pushed the key further towards me.

"The old woman has taken the children to Acre. She says to you: Here is the key. You'll find oil and tahina in the back room. There is a can of olives under the sofa cushions, and your clothes are in their place. As for the horse, they left him with the mukhtar." Opening the palm of my hand, he placed the axe in it. Then he left. I returned to the village when I heard that it had become a target for constant raids. Since it was impossible for the bus to get all the way to the village, I had to leave it some distance away. Because I knew the region perfectly, I began to push on into the thorns and bushes. After awhile I got rid of my suitcase. That particular May was hotter than usual and when I took off my coat, I remembered that I had hung the key from its pocket for fear that it might fall. So I also remember that when I entered the village three hours later at the end of the trip, I was carrying nothing but the key.

I knew that the perfect calm in the village concealed a potential ambush and so I began to walk close to the walls like a fugitive cat. When I was near the house Yahya jumped out in front of me. He was carrying a gun and he pulled me behind the wall. Without even greeting me, he asked: "You're late. Where's the key?"

He didn't let me savor the warmth of this "the" which had been returned now to the key to our house. For the past several weeks my friends in Jerusalem, whenever they saw the key on the table, would say: This is a key. That would always infuriate me, but I never said anything about it. As for Yahya though, with him the whole thing was warm and natural once again. He repeated:

"Where is the key?"

He didn't wait when he saw it in my hand, but took it, motioning with his head that I should follow him. When we had climbed the hill, he said to me: "The location of your house is excellent. And I remember that your mother left us a can of olives and some tahina."

The world was suddenly spinning round me once again. Your mother left us. I felt the warmth I had missed over the years when I had become used to it not being there and this only made me welcome it all the more. At the last minute Yahya got up all of a sudden and put the key back in my hand. His face reminded me of the day he had come to Jerusalem to tell me: "Your life is before you," but he said nothing. We went down the hill together in silence, he carrying his gun and me with the axe inside my head.

A piece of iron? This is the way many people saw it. It seems that my sister had found no place to put it and so had pounded two nails into the wall for it and quietly hung it directly above the radio. It was a large, beautiful, somewhat strange key. But for our guests it was nothing but a large, beautiful, strange key. The first nail went into its ring and the second one was placed under its head. The winds of twenty years passed over it and dust and rust had collected on it. But it was still there. It was a part of our new wall and I remember that once when my sister took it down to clean the dust off it, the room immediately seemed incomplete and cold and forsaken. Both my sister and I, with a simple exchange of looks, agreed that this was the case.

Day after day our key became only a key as far as many people were concerned, sometimes even as far as I was concerned. Did I say that we forgot it? Of course not, but it no longer reminded me of an axe. Sometimes I would sit and look at it for a long time and then I would ask myself: how could I ever have seen it as a small axe? How could my grandfather think that some colossal strength could change an axe into a key? When my son Hassan was born and saw it there, he probably saw it as a picture hanging on the wall. I waited for him to say to me one day that it looked like an axe, just as my father had waited for me to do the same thing. But it seems that that did not occur to him. And so I said to myself: what's the use anyway? what is it that I want?

Twenty Mays had passed. Not that that means anything, but May reminded me of something, something mysterious, like a nightmare. I said to myself: Time is a continuous stream and this is just a part of that time. It doesn't mean anything specific. The middle of May is just like the middle of any other month, just as one day is like any other day of the twenty years that have passed. And the days of the twenty years which have gone by, they don't mean anything in particular. But any given day has a bridge and a bridge has to have two sides, attached to something here and to something there . . . But a key is something else, it's something special and for me it can never be simply a key. It's true that it lost the warm "the" on the tongues of friends and visitors, but for my sister and myself, it never lost it, and we pronounced this "the" with special intensity so that it makes a sound like a door slamming.

I'll tell you now what happened to both the key and the middle of May together. It seems like a coincidence beyond the human mind's power to understand. But coincidences—at least as far as I'm concerned—are absolutely possible. And when it happened, I said to myself: How is it that all this time I didn't expect this to happen?

My sister came in one morning and turned on the radio. Hassan was sitting in the room eating his breakfast. It seems that my sister hadn't adjusted the volume and so suddenly the sound came on very loud, like thunder, and began to shake the tiny room. I was mostly trying to listen when one of the nails fell from under the key so that the body of the key fell and began to dangle back and forth from the nail which was still in its ring. This caught the attention of my sister and me and I felt a kind of trepidation which prevented me from speaking. It seemed that she felt the same trepidation. Meanwhile the key went on swinging, making a rustling sound like the wind. Hassan shouted, pointing with his finger to the key: "Look. It looks like an axe!"

—translated by Barbara Harlow

Suliman's Friend Learns
Many Things in One Night

E XACTLY LIKE AN EYE MOVING IN ITS SOCKET, THE
muzzle of the gun was pointed directly at his face. The
man carrying it looked like someone wearing a suit of
clothes that didn't belong to him. His bare arms were covered
with a blond down and on his head was a loosely strapped hel-
met. He wasn't exactly frightened, since he felt deeply that he
was innocent and that they weren't going to kill him. Even so he
was unable to concentrate his attention on any one thing.

When the muzzle moved slightly, like a finger indicating a
direction, he started walking slowly. The idea came to him: he
had learned that in the movies. Otherwise how could he have
understood that the almost imperceptible movement of the gun
was an order to start walking? And how could the soldier have
expected him to understand if he weren't sure that he had
learned it in the movies?

Afterwards he tried to remember a film in which he had
seen the same kind of scene, but he gave up the somewhat infu-
riating effort. He knew he had to think about something else
now. It all seemed so preposterous, as if some kind of magnet
fastened his head to this steel muzzle. Going out the door he
added a new detail to this thought of his. The soldier himself

113

was like a movie actor. And he said to himself: he learned that in the movies.

He was tempted by a desire to turn around and look at the soldier again, but he didn't dare. Instead he tried to form an image of him in his mind, exactly the way he had seen him for the first time, about twenty minutes earlier. Here he succeeded at least to the extent of being reassured that it was an image of a movie actor, and he said to himself: "It's practically unimaginable, it's as if his image were all ready to impress even the most distant spectators."

It caused him some pain that he was unable to get out of this frame of reference which was unnecessary for him now, but which was forcibly controlling his thoughts. His walking was monotonous and he decided that this must be what was preventing him from getting out of these monotonous thoughts which had nothing to do with his situation. So he stopped.

But nothing happened. The sounds of the footsteps on the stones behind went suddenly silent. A deep silence prevailed, throbbing with unrestrained expectation. From that abyss of emptiness he remembered a similar silence: the officer who was training him had said to him: Throw it! So he had pulled the fuse of the hand grenade and counted slowly to three. Then he threw it with his arm over his head as far as he could and watched the grenade hit the ground some distance away. It bounced heavily three times, then stopped. He waited a little while, his back bent and his arm still outstretched in front of him like a Greek statue. But the grenade just stayed there, still as a rock, dreadful, as if it were dead. The officer said to him: "It didn't go off." And he repeated, "No, it didn't go off." He remained standing there, not knowing what to do. A moment later he heard the officer say quietly: "Go get it." He turned around trying to force a half smile, but the officer was still frowning. Once again, he said: "Go get it. I told you to go." He thought: "It might go off." He walked about, but didn't go any closer. Finally he decided to say: "I'm not going to go. It could go off in my hand." He sighed deeply as if to relieve his chest of something heavy, but the officer shouted in a thundering voice: "Go get it. I'm telling you. That's an order. Move!" All the noise went silent around him. The men, exhausted from the drilling, crowded around, encircling him with their silence. He looked at them, all bathed in the silvery dust. Their heavy breathing came in muffled sounds. The grenade was there in the distance, a generation of stupidity away, as if outside the range of the game grounds. Under the scourge of the looks, he decided not to retreat: "No. I won't go. It's crazy." A faint clamor went up around him. The stones rattled under the officer's feet as he stepped back a few paces. Then suddenly something happened that he had not been expecting and the officer aimed the muzzle of his gun directly in his face, coldly ordering him: "I told you to go and get it." A bottomless abyss of silence opened, throbbing with unrestrained expectation.

*   *   *

The silence went on longer than he had anticipated, but nothing happened. The muscles of his back were tensed to the breaking point and trembling. He was expecting the muzzle of the gun to shove him forward, but nothing happened. For some time he couldn't quite work out if he should fall back on the magnetism of the rifle's steel which he could now feel directly on his back. He said to himself: "Just the way it happens in the movies." Then he said again: "He looks like an actor getting ready for a paid performance in front of a hidden camera." He made an effort to jump beyond the circle of his thoughts which he felt were irrelevant to the subject, saying to himself: the soldier is behind me. Behind him is probably my brother Riyadh. Then my mother. And a long row of people consisting of all the neighbors. The soldiers are standing among them and every one of them has his finger on the trigger. Do they all have their arms over their heads the way I do? Probably. Riyadh must look a little ridiculous since his arms are so short. The Israelis must think he's not reaching them as high as he should. What about mother?

When the muzzle of the gun suddenly jabbed him in the back, he took a few steps in spite of himself. The image of his mother fell out of his head and shattered and the pieces and splinters of it were strewn about. When he tried once more to stop, the muzzle shoved him forward again. He began to walk, trying not to think.

This, however, was impossible and a new idea exploded in his head: "As long as I can't stop, why not hurry? This will be just as inconvenient for the soldier." But he dismissed the idea, saying: "If I hurry, he'll fire." Presently he concluded something very important: "I'm safer the closer I am to the rifle, and the further I am from it, the more liable to death."

The idea surprised him and he smiled to himself, saying: "This is a new and excellent military principle. It's been demonstrated many times." It occurred to him in some mysterious way that the idea was all the more dangerous because of how simple it appeared, but was broader and deeper too. He admitted to himself: "It's coming very slowly."

*   *   *

"Very slowly." The officer was still pointing the muzzle of the gun at him and asking him to commit this fatal stupidity and pick up the grenade which hadn't exploded. Still he didn't move, but remained standing in the middle of the shower of expectant looks which his comrades, covered with the silvery dust, lashed out at him. Ever since he had entered this training course, they had been warning him about this officer who knew no mercy. He was prepared to kill. He wasn't really an officer, but that was what they all called him. He was nothing but a drill instructor. What was he going to do now?

Suddenly his friend Suliman came forward and spoke to the officer: "Will you allow me to solve the problem for you?" The officer nodded his head in agreement, glad to be rid of a dilemma which a moment before had seemed completely hopeless. Suliman stepped to the front and aiming his rifle at the grenade, fired it in a small volcano of stones and dust and smoke. The officer looked at him angrily: "You think very slowly. That is not appropriate for a *fida'i*. Do you understand? Inappropriate." Suliman started to polish his rifle, to avoid causing any more aggravation. His friend went back to the tent which the sun had roasted in a fabulous oven of dust. When he sat down there, he felt like crying.

*   *   *

"Sit down there." He sat down, putting his hands over his head. His mother sat down next to him, and behind the two of them sat Riyadh and the rest of the men. There were men, women and children, their eyelids still heavy with sleep, beginning to walk past in front of him. They were staggering, with their tiny hands raised limply, as if they were walking in their sleep. They sat down on piles of stones in the middle of a dark lake of silence.

His mother said to him in a whisper: "What are they going to do with us?" A soldier's voice came from behind: "Silence." Then he brought a light raised high on a rod. Other soldiers came and stood in front of them, like school teachers. One of them spoke: "You, did you see any of them?" Again his mother whispered: "The dog. And he speaks Arabic too." The soldier looked at her and their eyes met. Then he said: "You. Come here." Looking at another soldier standing next to him, he said: "I don't like him."

He stood up with his arms still raised, thinking: "They're in school. This is gym class and they're teaching us to get up without using our arms. It looks hard, so why is it so easy now?" He shook his head, trying to think clearly about the situation, but the idea kept coming back: "Man learns new things at strange moments, without even intending to." "Stop here." He stopped. "Raise your arms high." He raised his arms higher than he could. "Where were you two hours ago?" So this was the interrogation. He decided to be antagonistic and show that he knew how to proceed. He thought a bit and answered.

"Sleeping."

"You needed all that time to remember that you were sleeping? When I ask you a question, you answer fast. Do you understand?"

"I understand, si . . ."

He had been about to say "sir", but he couldn't do it and took a slight pleasure in the fact that the soldier hadn't noticed.

"Do you expect me to believe that? Can you prove that you were sleeping in your house?"

He motioned weakly with his head towards his mother sitting behind him, saying in a trembling voice: "Ask her. She's my mother."

"Were you sleeping with your mother, you son of a bitch?"

The soldiers laughed and so did one or two of the men sitting behind him. He thought: "That's the kind of laugh that comes from those who are asking to be set free, collaborators. But what else can they do?"

"Okay. Did you see anyone in the village last night?"

He thought: "Of course, you fool. Suliman."

"No."

"No one at all? Are you sure?"

"Yes, I'm sure. Everything was as usual."

"As usual? What's the usual?"

"You know. The usual."

When he had seen Suliman early in the evening, he had stood there in surprise, whereupon Suliman had said to him: "Don't stand there like an imbecile, man. Get yourself out of here." But instead he came forward and shook hands with him, asking after a short while: "What are you doing here?"

Suliman answered, laughing: "The usual."

The soldier shouted loudly.

"Listen, you fool. I just asked you . . . What's the usual? What's the village like when it's usual? Tell me!"

"Nothing, like every day."

"There were footprints, kid."

"We all walk."

He slapped him. The nearby hills gave out a sound like the tumbling of copper vessels. The soldier said: "If you keep on being stupid, you're going to find out what killing is. Also if you keep on being smart."

The sentence pleased him and he almost went on to plunge inside it, think about it and draw conclusions from it, conclusions that were more important than they had seemed at first glance. But the soldier interrupted this train of thought which always gave him such pleasure, saying:

"Listen, in a little while you're going to see how you should blow up houses. Not the way you do it . . . you don't even know how. But now we're going to teach you how to lift the house right from its very foundations with mines. You'll see how it will take off and drop like a glass ball."

He thought: "That's because you take your time. They are expecting us to take our time."

"Go back to your place."

He turned around—just as he had learned in the drill camp—without understanding why, and started walking, but before he had taken two steps the soldier called him back again.

"You walk like a soldier. Where did you learn to walk like that?"

Now he really sensed the danger. Behind him his mother let out a short scream. There was a strange aroma beginning to suffuse around him like a small tornado. He got himself together, feeling a sudden power envelop his body.

"Like a soldier? Not at all. I always walk like that. That's the way Allah made me."

"Allah made you like that? Allah made you?"

He thought angrily: "No. The officer's answer was better."

The day following the incident of the grenade, he had been standing in the morning battalion. Those who were assigned to take part in the "morning promenade" had to run at least five miles carrying their weapons and equipment. When with their first steps the ends of their guns, which were hanging from the men's shoulders, began to bang against the canteens of water attached to their hips, the officer had shouted: "Halt!" And they halted. Then he said: "You! Come here." He took two steps forward, out of the line. Looking at him the officer asked: "Aren't you the grenade man?"

"Yes, sir."

"Why are you walking so lazily, as if you were a pair of empty pants?"

"I always walk like that. That's the way Allah made me."

"No. You're wrong. The ones that Allah sent to this army, he made *fidayeen* from the beginning. Do you understand that? If Allah made you as lazy as you look, you would never have felt the need to come here . . . Now, stop blaming him for your mistakes."

"Blaming who, sir?"

"Allah."

Half-laughing, the soldier repeated: "Did Allah make you?"

"Yes."

"Okay. I believe you. But he made you to be truthful, didn't he? So let's be truthful, eh? Where were you trained to walk like that?"

"Right now, Mr. Soldier. From you."

"From me? You seem to be a man who thinks quickly. That doesn't please us very much."

"Yes."

"Yes what?"

"It doesn't please you very much."

His mind was completely clear now and he felt a kind of harmony with the things surrounding him. He began to wait, ignoring the words dispersed around him in the same way as a drizzling rain disperses when it encounters a powerfully gushing torrent. When he heard the order to go back to his place, he turned around and sat down next to his mother who reached out her hand and squeezed his arm, whispering: "Thank God, you're innocent."

The words pounded into him like a nail and he felt his body tremble. The following instant the words seemed to him meaningless and of no avail. They could be used in far different ways. He said to himself: "These same words have another meaning only three meters away, for that soldier over there covered with blond fuzz." He would have been able to pursue his thought further if he hadn't heard his mother asking him:

"What are they going to do now?"

"They're going to blow up the houses."

"Our houses?" "Our houses." "Why?" "Because I . . ." "Because of you?" "Because I'm innocent." It occurred to him that he might laugh, but that was impossible because the soldier was busy interrogating another man and he was afraid that his laughter would seem like an unworthy kind of connivance. Suddenly he remembered Suliman. He had been carrying a sack and now they were taking revenge for what he had done. Things were all mixed up in such a way that made even language nothing but a joke. He looked at his mother. "Do you remember Suliman?" "No." "Well, I remember him. He too gave his innocence." He was silent awhile, when suddenly he felt that his voice had taken on an interrogative tone, as if he were trying to discover unknown things.

"You hid my weapon and told me that I was crazy. I should have gone with Suliman."

"If you had done that, they would have torn down our houses."

He looked at her a moment. She seemed to be looking at him across the darkness, regretting the meaningless words she had just uttered. In his head there was no answer. The next instant an answer came from the horizon and a flash of lightning burst through the darkness. Then the echoes of wild thunder like demolitions inside their chests. On the hill they saw their houses collapse in the midst of torrents of smoke and flames. The noise of the explosions continued, destroying the stagnant night silence. He began to laugh, a laughter that filled his chest. The sound of thunder was so loud that the soldier did not hear him laughing. But his mother heard.

—translated by Barbara Harlow

Hamid Stops Listening to the Uncles' Stories

H E SLIPPED OUT FROM BETWEEN THE WIRES LIKE a cat. As'ad followed him feverishly, trying to do exactly what he did. But then I saw As'ad come to a stop, leaving him alone. I thought I heard whispering and As'ad appeared to be a kind of dark spectre moving about excitedly in his place. Hamid had gone much closer, more than was appropriate for a trained man like him. It was impossible to stop him. After a short while, he disappeared from our sight and there was a roar of thunder and a burst of firing that made you stiffen.

As'ad returned first. Then came Hamid. I began to run towards them, feeling the rifle's steel hotter in my hand than before. We roamed with silent steps about the dark rugged terrain.

As'ad said: "I'm getting closer. The splinters could kill you."

There was no answer. Meanwhile the darkness for some reason grew more intense. I noticed that Hamid was walking directly behind me, practically touching me. At first I just ignored him, but then I said to him: "Get away from me. Did you forget?"

He didn't answer. In my mind I formulated two decisive points which would have to be written down that night. Hamid had committed two serious violations. First of all, he had gone much too close to the tank. Then he had continued to hang on to me ignoring all the lessons which said that it was necessary to walk ten meters away from the nearest man and be careful of surprises.

Again I told Hamid: "Keep your distance from me." I saw his two silent eyes watching me. He stood quietly, directly behind me, carrying his heavy weapon. His gasping made a frightful sound. When I took a step, he took a step, wary of those few things that were separating us.

Finally I stopped and looked around angrily. Before I could say anything, he had already begun in a voice somewhat higher than it should be.

"I still don't hear."

"What?"

He didn't answer, and to myself I began to reconstruct the whole picture: when his bomb had exploded so close by, he had been deafened by the thunderous roar. This was a common occurrence that we had been told about and that we all knew. How could he not have thought of it?

I took his hand and placed it on my belt indicating to him that he should follow me. A little while later when we sat down to rest he put his hands to his ears and began to shake his head violently, saying hopelessly: "At night a *fida'i* is nothing but ears. He sees with his ears."

He put his fingers back in his ears, digging frenziedly into them. I looked at him sitting between As'ad and myself. He was practically not there at all.

Suddenly As'ad laughed and began to shake Hamid by the shoulders.

"Why did you go so close to the edge?"

Of course he didn't hear, but he smiled, probably feeling a sudden estrangement. I told As'ad: "Don't laugh at the poor man . . . Leave him to his worry. He's suffering."

"But why did he go so close to the edge of the tank? He could have smashed it from a hundred meters away. Why did he go so close?"

"I don't know. Ask him."

"But he doesn't hear."

"Maybe your question isn't important to him."

"My question's not important just because he doesn't hear? Nonsense!"

"Come on, let's go. They're following us."

We got up and Hamid put his fingers through my belt. He began watching the ground, being careful to place his steps in the footprints which I left.

In the darkness I reflected on what we were going to have to do with Hamid when we got him home. Probably lots of problems find solutions that you never thought about. Suddenly Hamid said to me: "Did you see how it collapsed, just like paper. A tongue of fire almost burned me."

"Did you want reassurance? Is that why you went so close?"

"The whole thing exploded, like a box of matches."

"Did you have doubts about how good your gun was?"

"Like paper. It started to burn."

The conversation was useless and I signalled him to be quiet. The skies had begun to drizzle and a flash of lightning fissured the horizon once or twice. I was sure we would arrive safely and so I could have ordered As'ad and Hamid both to go home. But I couldn't leave Hamid. I said to As'ad: "Let's go to my house."

*   *   *

First we hid our rifles, then we went on up together. My uncle, who was visiting us, greeted me coldly. He shook hands with the two guests with the tips of his fingers, trying to make them feel that late night guests were not wanted.

Nonetheless we sat down without paying any attention. My wife brought in tea which we drank. She asked me pointedly, as was her custom, why did I have to lie.

"You've been staying late in the coffeehouse. Did Hamid beat you at backgammon as usual?" She looked at Hamid.

"Did you beat him again this time?"

Hamid smiled, looking around him nervously. As'ad said: "I beat them both."

My uncle looked at us suspiciously, then at our shoes, without noticing anything. Finally he spoke.

"These days it's wise for a man to go to sleep early. He's supposed to be in his house before dark."

As'ad replied: "We were having fun. What's a man supposed to do at home all evening?"

"You're right. But it's better—I mean, I'm talking about safety—for a man to avoid problems. You know."

My wife tried to change the subject, but she chose the wrong topic. Turning to Hamid, she asked him: "How is Lamia?"

Hamid looked at the floor, preoccupied with searching for something which hadn't fallen from his hand. My uncle noticed this movement and addressed him.

"I don't think she's an admirer of backgammon evenings under these circumstances, do you, Mr. Hamid?"

I interrupted: "All wives are like that. Don't embarrass him."

"One of these days you'll walk out of the coffeehouse and they'll arrest you for some explosion that has taken place in a neighboring village. The devils won't let you out of their hands . . . and then no wife will be happy."

"You're right."

"I'm only interested in your welfare. These things require wisdom."

"Right."

"You're still young and you don't know how you're supposed to behave. If I were in your place, I would go."

"Go where?"

"Anywhere outside this hell."

"That's another topic."

"No, that is the topic. I think Mr. Hamid here agrees with me, because he's not blushing the way you and your friend are. Isn't that so, Mr. Hamid?"

Hamid, of course, hadn't heard. He had gone too close to the tank when he blew it up. He still didn't hear.

"Isn't that so, Mr. Hamid?"

I stretched out in my chair. Despite all my silent efforts, I lost my nerve and said to him: "Hamid doesn't hear you."

"He doesn't hear me?"

"No. Fortunately for him. He was struck by a sudden illness in his ears which saved him from having to listen. You know? So now he doesn't hear what you are saying, and he doesn't hear what they say. He only hears himself. So it's impossible, it's just wasting his time. Tomorrow you will hear on the radio about an attack made by unknown culprits on an army camp. But the attack was a failure and didn't cause any damage. You and I and As'ad, we'll hear that. But Hamid won't hear it. That's his good luck. He heard only one sound, and finally, it's the one sound which is going to stay in his memory."

His patience exhausted, my uncle said: "I don't understand any of this. Have you been drinking? All this talk of yours is just guessing games."

"Listen, uncle. There's a story which I'm going to tell you, right in front of Hamid. For the first time. This is my chance to tell it, because he won't hear it.

"He had a younger sister, twenty years ago, when they lived in a mosque because they had lost everything. He was just a child when his sister disappeared.

"His sister stayed away for a week or two while at home he heard strange and frightening things about her which he didn't completely understand. Then one day he saw her in the road, much more elegant than necessary, and with a strange man. He grabbed her by the leg. In trying to get away from him she dragged him along the pavement for about five metres, with him bleeding all the way. But he didn't let go of her and brought her back to the house.

"The result of all this was terrifying. The boy's leg became dangerously infected afterwards because the deep cuts caused by dragging him along the pavement all that distance while he was hanging on to his sister's leg were not treated.

"So Hamid remained there on the floor of the mosque which had become the home of at least twenty families.

"That was twenty years ago. Hamid was only six years old at

the time. For a long time he lay on his shabby bed and all that while he listened to the endless stories. Stories about old men and mothers and children. Fear and shame and lamentation. Helplessness and loss. Surrender. The uncles' stories, about wisdom and circumstances. For four years he listened. He listened a lot, a whole lot. In everything he listened to, there was one truth and that was that his sister had run away from home. She was lost.

"I tell you, he listened a lot, a whole lot. In that place filled with shame and defeat and ruin, there was nothing but an ear to hear, to listen to the echoes of words and stories and lamentation which couldn't destroy even a single fly, couldn't even bury one truth. His sister was gone.

"Now Hamid has decided to stop listening."

My uncle looked at Hamid, with a slight feeling of distress. Hamid, however, looked him in the face, silently, as if he were a stone. Then he looked at me, since I was the one who knew. His ears were filled, still, with a thunder that never subsided. The whole world had vanished behind that sound which no one heard but him.

I said to Hamid: "Don't worry. It will pass in a few days, maybe a week, and your hearing will come back. But you'll never forget that sound. It's the one sound which will bury everything left and cover it over."

In the street the heavy shoes of soldiers began to pound methodically. The sound came suddenly, as if it were coming from the room above. I looked at my uncle who was trembling.

We all looked at Hamid who had begun to move his eyes from one to the other of us, smiling from inside his private world. He heard there only the sound of mountains of steel collapsing.

Deeply uneasy, even down to his toes, my uncle asked: "Don't you hear?"

As'ad answered quietly: "Ask Hamid."

—*translated by Barbara Harlow*

Guns in the Camp

T HINGS CHANGE SUDDENLY, AND WHEN ABU SAAD stopped going to the coffeehouse, his conversation with Umm Saad became gentler. The morning that he asked her if she was still tired, he had smiled slowly when she looked at him, as if, in turn, to ask the reason for his question. He always used to come in exhausted, gruffly demanding his dinner and then nearly falling asleep in the middle of it.

When he was out of work, his gruffness only got worse and he would take to going to the coffeehouse where he drank tea and played backgammon and scolded everybody. When he came home, he was unbearable and would fall asleep with his big rough hands covered with dust and cement under his head, snoring loudly. In the morning he argued with his shadow, leaving Umm Saad to get her few things ready to go to work under the scathing glare of his inexplicable anger. One day Umm Saad could smell wine on his breath.

But now all that had suddenly changed. Now when he heard muffled footsteps passing in front of the windows of his little house, even though the narrow muddy passage was only wide enough for one person, he would get up, and, showing his face at the window, begin a conversation with the passerby, asking all kinds of questions and discussing the Kalashnikovs which he preferred to refer to simply as "Klash," the way Saad did whenever he came to visit them.

In the afternoon he would go to where an amplifier was broadcasting a speech, the likes of which he had never heard before. He stood there by the wall, watching, as if stricken with dismay, while the children in the camp, and the girls and the men too, were all either leaping through the rifle fire or crawling underneath the wires and brandishing their weapons. He watched Said, his youngest son, giving instructions before the gathering on what a combatant should do to avoid being wounded when resisting an attack.

When Said had gone down among the throng, the people had begun to clap. Umm Saad came and stood next to her husband on the low roof, looking off towards the open square. As soon as she had picked out Said, she let out a long trilling sound which was answered by other trills of joy from up and down the square. Abu Saad said to her: "Wait . . . do you see him? Keep an eye on him." As if she didn't see him! As if she weren't right there with him at the very heart of the crowd, counting the beads of sweat which soaked his small tanned brow.

Step by step Said drew near his adversary, his small hands clenched and leaning forward ever so slightly. Abu Saad placed his hand on his wife's shoulder, squeezing it with uncontained affection. Tears sprang to the eyes of Umm Saad as she fixed her attention wholly on Said.

Like a peal of thunder the clapping reverberated in the open square of the camp when Said managed to duck out of the way of a bayonet thrust. In the twinkling of an eye the child grabbed the gun from the hands of his opponent. He spun round and with his small arm raised the gun high, under the fluttering flag which gave off a sound like the clapping of hands.

Abu Saad applauded loudly. He stood upright and looked proudly about him. His eyes met the eyes of Umm Saad and leaning forward he said to her: "Did you see him? That's Said!"

He pointed to the child and brought his head close to hers so that she could see where he was pointing. His words grew stronger: "There he is! He's the one lifting the rifle. Do you see him?" So as not to burst out laughing, Umm Saad trilled again loud and joyously. The clapping continued while the child waved his gun in the face of the men crowded about. His forehead shone in the light of the setting sun, when suddenly an old man who was sitting on the edge of the wall looked at Abu Saad and said: "If only it had been like this from the beginning, nothing would have happened to us."

Abu Saad agreed, surprised at the tears which he saw in his old neighbor's eyes. "If only it had been like this from the beginning."

He came back, and taking the old man by the shoulder pointed with his outstretched arm to the middle of the square: "Do you see the boy holding the rifle? Well, that's my son, Said. Do you see him?"

Probably without seeing too well at all, the old man answered: "God bless you, young man."

Abu Saad raised his head slightly and went on talking to the old man. "His older brother Saad is with the *fidayeen* up in the caves."

Abu Saad pulled his wife towards him. Pointing to her, he said to the old man who was still looking into the square: "This woman has borne two sons who have grown up to become *fidayeen*. She provides the children for Palestine."

At that the old man looked at Umm Saad, who, even though she was laughing, never took her eyes off Said who had returned the rifle to his comrade and was hurrying to catch up with the long line of children dressed in khaki standing at the far end of the square.

Abu Saad changed that afternoon. That's what Umm Saad told me. "Of course," she said, "the situation changed . . . the young man told me that life would taste good from now on."

Umm Saad said: "Just look at the boys in the camp. Everyone is carrying a rifle or a machine gun, and there's a soldier in every house. Do you see what Saad has done?"

"What does Saad have to do with this?"

"What do you mean? Do you really think all this happened just by chance? If you only knew, cousin. A rifle is like the measles. The peasants say that when a child gets measles, this means that he has begun to live, and that his life is guaranteed. The day when I saw Saad carrying a rifle, I said to the effendi who was strolling past me that morning: 'You made your money. That's over now.' On Wednesday the effendi was the first to walk outside the camp. The camp went wild, as if someone had put a match to a haystack. Just look at the boys and you'll see."

"And Abu Saad?"

Umm Saad clapped her hands. They sounded to me almost like two pieces of wood being struck together. "The poor, cousin . . . the poor . . . The poor can change an angel into a devil or the devil into an angel. What could Abu Saad do except lose his temper and take it out on the people and on me and on his own shadow. Abu Saad had been crushed. Crushed by the poor, crushed by the victors, crushed by the ration card, crushed under a tin roof, crushed under the domination of the country . . . What could he do? Saad's going restored his spirits and that day he was a little better. He saw the camp in another way. He lifted his head and began to look around. He looked at me and he looked at his children differently. Do you understand? If you could just see him now, strutting around like a rooster. He can't see a gun on a young man's shoulder without moving aside and caressing it, as if it were his own old gun that had been stolen and he had just now found it again."

She stopped a moment, thinking about what she had said, like someone remembering something, but suddenly she went on: "This morning he woke up very early. When I looked for him outside, I saw him standing in the road smoking a cigarette and leaning up against the wall. Even before wishing me good morning, he said: 'Allah, Umm Saad, look at us, we're alive.'"

The room filled with the fragrance of deep-rooted countryside when Umm Saad took her little bundle and turned towards the door. I was afraid that she had gone, but then I heard her voice coming through the two open doors. "The grapevine is blooming, cousin! The grapevine is blooming!"

I stepped towards the door where Umm Saad was bent over the dirt, where there grew—since a time when at that moment seemed to me infinitely remote—the strong firm stems which she had brought to me one morning. A green head sprouting through the dirt with a vigor that had a voice of its own.

—translated by Barbara Harlow

He Was a Child That Day

T HE BLAZING REDNESS OF THE MORNING SUN anointed the sands of the silver coast. The twisted date trees shook last night's sleep from their languid idle fronds and stretched their thorny arms skyward to where the walls of Acre towered above the dark blueness. To the right was the road coming from Haifa. To the left the large round disc of the sun climbed into view from behind the hills and tinged the tops of the trees, the water, and the road with the blushing hue of early morning shyness. Ahmad took a reed flute from the basket and leaning back in the corner of the car began to blow into it an injured air of rebuke, of an eternal lover. He might live in any one of the villages scattered like the still stars throughout the land.

The bus, however, was hiding in the breezes of the sunrise. The injured melody came naturally to an end, which was precisely the reason that nobody in the corners of the car was in any way surprised by the song. They expected the song to burst forth from out of everything around them. The surprise was in actually finding it missing.

The fields wandered off to the left, undulating with blood-stained green, the waves continuing their eternal efforts to mount the silver sand. In all that small enduring mineral world, the service taxi, with its melody of grief, was a kind of unseen and unspoken link joining twenty men who had never in their lives, until that morning's greeting while they waited for the taxi in King Faisal Street in Haifa, exchanged a word with each other.

This world was a small one, made up of workers, absorbed by the docks like a faulty siphon, from all the holes of Galilee and peasants from the district of Haifa, related by marriage from a time before their memories, men and women from the district of Safad, and one child from Umm al-Faraj, whose mother had sent him to Haifa to see if his father was still alive and who was returning now with the answer. There was the whole legal issue of land in al-Kabri and the lawyer whose job it was to inquire into this before the courts. There was a woman trying to match a young girl with her only son. There were baskets filled with food, flat bread and pigeons baked in brick ovens, children's toys and whistles, and letters that were being carried from one distant place to another, between those who had fled. There was the reed flute belonging to the young man whose school had been closed only the day before. And the driver who knew the road like he knew his own wife.

From Haifa, along the winding road which clung to the coast like a necklace, ascending wherever the palm trees sprang forth and retreating in confusion in its silent agonizing struggle with the old irrigation canal from the sea. Above the river al-Na'amin which flowed sadly and wearily, but pure still, in a noisy torrent, with stubborn calm. From there the car climbed the road to Acre, to al-Manshiah, to al-Samaria, to al-Mazra'a, to Nahariya, turning east and plunging through dozens of villages, leaving along the road a passenger here, a basket there, a letter for a man who is waiting and a husband for a woman who couldn't wait.

One of the men spoke to another who was sitting next to him: "This young man is a good flute player." The other man didn't answer. He was looking out the window, absorbed in the melody, as if it were a jar of the choicest cream.

The child laid his head in the lap of the old woman sitting

next to him and fell asleep. Another woman, who didn't know him, had prepared flat bread stuffed with boiled eggs, and was waiting for him to wake up so she could give him something to eat. The driver hummed a song along with the melody, about a young man who was able to carry a mountain and place it on the house of the girl he loved, just in case she wanted to flee to the cave where there was a mat, a loaf of bread and olive pits. Acre was approaching, through the windows. First the cemetery on the right side of the road, then the station to the left, and a little further on houses built of Jerusalem stone, puffed like loaves of bread. Behind them were the walls of the "public garden," yellow with its tall quinine trees. In the distance appeared the tops of the wall with its brown stone towers and the green plants growing from their crevices. On the left there were new houses, small and planted round with row upon row of luxuriant jujube blossoms. On the horizon was Tel al-Fakhar, venerable with its flat summit and its peaceful verdant surface with the tombs of soldiers whose resistance had bequeathed them death and who now saw no further than the walls. Then to the left, the quarantine building, and a string of repair shops which never slept, but watched over rows of tires rising higher and higher like barrels in front of their grease-stained doors. Dusty vines and plants climbed over the wrecks of cars awaiting repairs, or weighing, or simply eaten with rust.

A man took off his coat and covered the child with it. Another man, named Salah, took an orange from his basket, peeled it and offered it first to his neighbor, as etiquette and custom required. Two other men were discussing the olive season, while a corpulent woman who had made the pilgrimage the year before was now telling a story about how the Jews had blown up an orphanage in Jaffa and how the bodies of the children had been strewn about the crater of Iskandar Iwad Street mixed with the seeds of burst oranges. A bomb had been placed in a truck filled with oranges which was stopped at the steps of the orphanage. A turbaned shaykh had declared that the hand of Allah would smite all those who killed orphans. Allah would surely take his vengeance now.

Five minutes before Nahariya the child woke up. The sun

was blazing, and one of the men was getting ready to leave the car. At the edge of the road, there was a cart carrying vegetables pulled by a small white donkey. The reed pipe was silent now, and in a loud voice the driver said: "God willing, let it be something good!" The men surveyed the road from atop the back of the driver's seat. Ahmad said, "It's a patrol," but Salah corrected him: "No, they're Jews." The hajja exclaimed: "Oh my God." Then the car stopped and the driver turned off the engine.

"Get out," said a soldier dressed in dark green and carrying a machine gun. He poked his head inside. The driver got out first, holding the child, then the women, and finally, after everyone else, came the men.

The men were the first to be searched, then the baskets were torn apart and the carefully knotted white bags opened. The two soldiers who carried out this operation reported to their officer, a short tanned man with a revolver strapped around his waist and carrying a black stick, that the baskets and bags had no weapons in them.

This short officer ordered a soldier standing next to him to call the child, then he indicated with a circular gesture to his men that they should start lining up the men and women at the side of the road with the stream of water directly behind them. He proceeded to count them and announced in Hebrew: fifteen.

He struck his leg lightly with his black stick, while the child standing next to him paid no attention to any of it. With short resolute steps he passed up and down in front of the expectant line and began:

"This is war, you Arabs . . . you say you're so brave, and you call us mice. You, come here." A girl appeared from behind a small car. She was wearing shorts and had a machine gun slung over her shoulder. She stood with her bare legs spread apart on the other side of the road.

"This is your quota for today."

They fell into the ditch, their hands and faces sunk in the mud, collapsed in a dense, confused and bloody heap. Blood ran underneath their bodies, combining with the water from the stream flowing towards the south.

The tanned man looked at the child. Leaning towards him, he took his ear cruelly between his fingers: "You see? Remember this well when you tell the story . . ." He straightened up, and cuffing the child from behind with his black stick, pushed him forward. "Let's go. Run as fast as you can. I'm going to count to ten and if you aren't out of here by then I'm going to shoot."

The terrified child couldn't believe any of it and remained fixed on the spot like one of the trees planted around him. His jaw dropped showing his imperfect teeth, as he looked from the ditch to the girl with her shorts. The next instant he had received another blow with the black stick and felt it cut his flesh. There was nothing for him to do but throw his legs to the wind and take off down the road, a veil of dizziness, mist and tears before his eyes.

Through it all the sound of their loud laughter reached his ears and he stopped. He didn't understand what had happened or why, but he stopped. Putting his hands in his trouser pockets, and without looking back, he walked with quiet deliberate steps down the middle of the road. He began to count slowly to himself: one, two, three . . .

—*translated by Barbara Harlow*

Six Eagles and a Child

I WAS WORKING AT THE TIME AS A MUSIC TEACHER IN the villages . . . In those days it wasn't actually necessary for a music teacher to understand music. All he had to do was sing songs for the children, and then when they were all asked to sing together, he had to keep the rhythm under control.

The work would not have been at all demanding . . . if—on account of the subject I was teaching—I didn't have to travel between three villages in order to give lessons in each of them. For the first couple of months, I really felt as though I was something special, but even these feelings vanished entirely as soon as I took my place in the ancient car which was used as a service taxi, sitting in the middle of the peasants and driving across the rugged terrain . . . it was unbearable . . . But on top of that I had begun to feel that the work I was doing was nothing but the slow burial of all the aspirations I had carried with me the day I graduated from secondary school.

The trip in the taxi was something awful! Occasionally I would try to sleep on the way, but the rough bouncing of the car always came between me and what I was doing. The few times that I felt like I was about to fall asleep in spite of it all, I would be jolted back to reality by a basket, or a watermelon, or something else which the man sitting next to me had shoved into my lap . . . or else I would wake up in a panic at being kicked by my neighbor who was hoping thereby to get me to come in as an arbiter in the dispute between him and his companion.

I put up with all this grudgingly . . . because of the position the schoolteacher holds in the villages . . . The schoolteacher there is something holy . . . and it would have been too bad for any of us to break down that special holiness of ours with some momentary grumbling or a crude word . . . so we just shook our heads whenever we were dragged into some dispute, or smiled benignly when a peasant wanted us to give him a hand . . .

As a result I put up with all this grudgingly . . . but the one thing that could really break down all my dignified reserve, was when a peasant would give me a nudge in that old car rocking and hurtling over the rough mountain road. Those were the moments that were supposed to be my free time between one class and another. Then I was expected to take part in the conversation and show an interest for the rest of the way.

"Do you see that rock, professor?" said an old peasant one day, pointing through the window to a tall tapering stone standing on a small hill . . .

"Yes . . . in fact I see it three times a week . . ."

His fingers remained extended in the direction of the rock and he asked again: "Do you know its story?"

"Does this rock have a story?" I asked out of curiosity, since even though I knew full well that everything in the villages had a story, I didn't know that this rock, way out here on this desolate road, had its story too. Nonetheless, my question had a certain grumbling to it, and raising the newspaper in front of my eyes, I began to read it desultorily.

"It began a long time ago . . ."

I ignored him and went on reading, certain that the old peasant wasn't looking at me, but was gazing at the rock as it slowly disappeared from the window's range of vision.

"I used to travel this way every other day . . . and always when I passed this rock I would see a grey eagle perched on top of it as if it were some kind of stuffed eagle . . . it was in the morning . . . spreading its enormous wings, it would fly to the

top of the rock and then alight quietly. It remained there like
that until evening when it would fly off again to return to the
mountains . . ."

I folded the newspaper and, putting it in my pocket, I
looked at the old man's face. It was as if he were talking to one
of his children: "For six whole months it didn't miss a day."

"Do you know why?"

He looked at me all of a sudden, as if he were seeing me for
the first time . . . He hesitated a moment before turning back to
the window and answering my question: "No one knows why
animals do what they do . . . but anyway this particular eagle
was born on that rock. Its mother was quite old and couldn't lay
her egg in the mountains and so she left it here. Then, when the
egg broke and the baby bird hatched, the mother died. The
eaglet remained on the rock."

He turned from the window and looked at me: "When the
eagle had grown, he felt his time was approaching . . . and he
began to come every day to the place where his mother died . . .
waiting . . ."

"Did he die?"

"Yes . . . there came a day when I didn't find him there anymore."

I opened my newspaper again and started to read, but the
old man had not yet finished his story. "The eagle is a faithful
animal . . ."

I shook my head, and the old man looked at me with
approval at my assent in his eyes. All the while he stared at me I
could think of nothing to say but to repeat: "Yes, the eagle is a
faithful animal . . ."

On the way back there was a young peasant sitting next to
me holding a huge basket of corn. At first we just exchanged a
few brief words, but then just when we were passing in front of
the rock, he tapped me on the shoulder and pointed at it
through the window. He was just about to start when I cut him
off. "God have mercy on the eagle! You know his story, of course
. . . He was faithful . . ."

He lowered his hand to his leg and shook his head sorrowfully: "Love . . . love does that to everyone . . ."

"Love?"

"She must have loved him . . ."

"Who?"

He looked at me in curiosity and shouted: "Why, the female eagle that died . . . It seems you don't know the story after all . . ."

He straightened up in his seat so that he was looking right at me and threw his heavy basket of corn on my knees: "She used to come every morning and circle about above the rock before alighting. She stayed until sunset and then returned with the twilight to the mountains."

I sighed and asked impatiently: "Why is that?"

"It's a long story . . . They say that two male eagles once fought over her on this rock . . . from faraway you could hear their shrieking and they pecked away at each other until their blood flowed. Finally one of them killed the other . . . But the female eagle didn't love the victor . . . and so on, so that the poor eagle got into another fight, this time with her, and she beat him badly. The second victim fell next to his rival . . ."

"Then what?"

He pointed vaguely to the rear to where the rock had gone and shook his head painfully: "Then she started to cry for both of them on top of the rock and she cried until she died."

"Do you know how she died?"

"Most probably she stopped eating . . ."

He turned and straightened up in his seat and began to look out the window at the desolate hills, saying almost in a whisper: "The female eagle is a cruel animal . . ."

A week went by and I had almost forgotten the two stories . . . when I was reminded of them by a middle-aged woman in a loose-flowing dress who was sitting next to me: "If her husband had been in her place, would he have done the same thing?"

She pointed to the rock, looking at me like someone wanting to persuade me to accept his opinion: "Who knows? And he might do as she did . . . after all, didn't he die for her sake?"

"For her sake?"

I asked beseechingly but she shook her head: "They always came here, the two of them . . . I used to see them every week, whenever I travelled, bickering quietly with each other and whimpering like two kittens . . . I was still engaged to Abu al-Hassan, and so I used to watch them closely every time I passed by here. Then, after a while, I found her standing there alone . . . Probably he flew away from her . . ."

I laughed and asked jokingly: "Why do you think he flew away from her?"

"You're all like that . . . eagles too . . . Maybe he found himself another little one and so he left her."

She looked at me in agitation and slapped my leg: "Do you see? After he left, she continued to come every day . . . standing . . . waiting . . . shrieking, until she died . . ."

"How did she die?"

"From grief, of course."

Once this woman got out, I was alone in the taxi . . . But the driver wouldn't leave me in peace. He pointed to the rock, and started shouting over the rumbling of the engine: "They tell many stories about the eagle that used to stand on that rock, but its all just imagination . . . The eagle used to stand here because his nest was here. Then it was moved."

I leaned forward so he could hear me and shouted my question: "Why?"

"In the days when he used to stand there I was working with only one other colleague. We didn't make much noise on the road with our passing . . . But then there came to be a lot more cars, most of them running on mazut, and the smoke from mazut is really bad, and the noise is even worse, and so he didn't return to the rock, which was no longer suitable, but fled from his nest to the mountains."

Time passed, a week at the most, in which I didn't travel at all, because of a sudden illness. When I had recovered my strength enough to be able to go back to work, there was a new passenger sharing the taxi with me. He was an improvement in that he didn't talk. He was new at working in the villages and so he kept to the road in silence, which pleased me . . . But when we passed by the stone, I grew impatient with the silence, and had no objection to talking, so I tapped him: "Look . . . see that rock? Well, you're going to hear a lot of stories about it in the future . . . stories having to do with an eagle."

"An eagle?"

"Yes."

He was silent and it occurred to me that he might be about to fall asleep, so I returned to the conversation: "I think it was a small eagle. It came here every day and stayed until evening. That's because his little wings couldn't carry him to a higher rock. When he got a little bigger he found himself a higher spot."

My companion shook his head. It seemed to me that he didn't want to have a conversation and was going back to sleep.

On the way back, one of my old travelling companions joined me . . . During all that time, the rock had become a characteristic of the road and of conversation. As we passed by it, I turned to my companion: "Do you know anything about that rock?"

"Only that it's a contemporary of mine."

"How so?"

"Ever since I was fired from my old job because of my political activities, I've been working here . . . so I know all the stories about the eagle . . ."

"Which do you think is the truest?"

He stretched out in his seat . . . and looked languidly out the window: "The eagle came here because he wanted to come here. There's no mystery about it . . . Why does a butterfly light on one flower and not on another? It's the same story . . . he came, stopped and then quietly went back to his nest."

"But they say that he died."

"Yes, killed . . ."

He indicated with his outstretched finger a white hut about ten meters away from the rock: "Before the police built this outpost, the eagle came every day. Then when they built it, it continued to come, except that one day one of the men on patrol killed him with his revolver, because, it's said, he was annoying him with his shrieking and crying."

"Did the bullet hit him?"

He nodded his head and went back to looking at the hut. Then he whispered: "It hit him, but it didn't kill him . . . He tried to fly but couldn't keep on until he was high enough, and he fell down into the valley."

Winter came and the service taxis changed their route, tak-ing another road which was not so snowy . . . Throughout the winter months I heard no more talk about the rock and the eagle . . . Then when spring came the taxis went back to the old road . . .

I didn't quite understand . . . was the reason for my forget-ting about the rock that there had been no talk about it, or did the road in spring take on a delusive appearance which attract-ed all one's attention . . . whatever it was . . . it was many days before I looked out of the car window and, without expecting it, saw the rock . . . I saw an enormous eagle on top of it, with folded grey wings, standing like something stuffed and looking in the direction of the road.

"The eagle is back . . ."

I said this in the tone of a journalist reporting a major piece of news and tapped the shoulder of my companion, who was only a child, motioning with my head towards the rock . . .

"What eagle?" the child asked innocently, looking towards where I was pointing . . . I stretched my hand outside the win-dow, directing his gaze again.

"The one standing on top of that rock . . . Don't you know his story?"

"That rock?"

"Yes."

He looked at me smiling uncomprehendingly. I nodded my head, pointing all the while towards the rock: In the meantime the child studied my face before saying slowly: "This isn't an eagle . . . look again . . . every spring a mulberry bush grows behind the rock and then in summer it dies or else the rabbits come and devour it before it dies."

I looked again . . . and it occurred to me that the child was telling the truth. Even so, I didn't want to give up and so I asked with some hesitation: "Are you sure?"

He smiled again, quite enjoying the sight of such an igno-rant teacher, and assured me with his small hands: "When the mulberries are ripe, I come with my friend to steal them . . . They're really delicious . . ."

—translated by Barbara Harlow

Returning to Haifa

1 When he reached the edge of Haifa, approaching by car along the Jerusalem road, Said S. had the sensation that something was binding his tongue, compelling him to keep silent, and he felt grief well up inside of him. For one moment he was tempted to turn back, and without even looking at her he knew that his wife had begun to cry silently. Then suddenly came the sound of the sea, exactly the way it used to be. Oh no, the memory did not return to him little by little. Instead, it rained down inside his head the way a stone wall collapses, the stones piling up, one upon another. The incidents and the events came to him suddenly and began to pile up and fill his entire being. He told himself that Safiyya, his wife, felt exactly the same, and that was why she was crying.

Ever since he left Ramallah that morning he had not stopped talking, nor had she. Beneath his gaze, the fields sped by through the windshield, and the heat was unbearable. He felt his forehead catch fire, exactly like the burning asphalt beneath the car's wheels, while above him the sun, the terrible June sun, spilled the tar of its anger upon the earth.

All along the way he talked and talked and talked. He spoke to his wife about everything—about the war and about the

149

defeat, about the Mandelbaum Gate, demolished by bulldozers. And about the enemy, who reached the river, then the canal, then the edge of Damascus in a matter of hours.[1] And about the ceasefire, and the radio, and the way the soldiers plundered belongings and furniture, and the curfew, and his cousin in Kuwait consumed with anxiety, and the neighbor who gathered his things and fled, and the three Arab soldiers who fought alone for two days on the hill near Augusta Victoria Hospital, and the men who took off their army uniforms and fought in the streets of Jerusalem, and the peasant who was killed the minute they saw him near the largest hotel in Ramallah. His wife spoke of many other matters. Throughout the entire journey neither of them stopped talking. Now, as they reached the entrance to Haifa, they both fell silent. At that moment they both realized that they had not spoken a word about the matter which had brought them there.

This is Haifa, then, twenty years later.

Noon, June 30, 1967. The car, a gray Fiat bearing white Jordanian license plates, was traveling north, across the plain which was called Ibn Amar twenty years ago.[2] It ascended the coastal road toward the southern entrance to Haifa. When the car crossed the road and entered the main street, all the walls came down and the road dissolved behind a film of tears. He heard himself say to his wife, "This is Haifa, Safiyya!"

The steering wheel felt heavy between his palms, which had begun to sweat more profusely than they ever had before. It occurred to him to say to his wife, "I know this Haifa, but it refuses to acknowledge me." However, he changed his mind and after a moment a thought struck him, and he said to her:

"You know, for twenty long years I always imagined that the Mandelbaum Gate would be opened some day, but I never, never imagined that it would be opened from the other side. It never entered my mind. So when they were the ones to open it, it seemed to me frightening and absurd and to a great degree humiliating. Maybe I'd be crazy if I told you that doors should always open from one side only, and that if they opened from the other side they must still be considered closed. But nevertheless, that's the truth."

He turned toward his wife, but she wasn't listening. She was turned away from him, absorbed in gazing at the road—now to the right, where the farmland stretched away as far as one could see, and now to the left, where the sea, which had remained so distant for more than twenty years, was raging near at hand. Suddenly she said:

"I never imagined that I would see Haifa again."

He said:

"You're not seeing it. They're showing it to you."

With that, Safiyya's nerves failed her for the first time and she shouted:

"What's all this 'philosophy' you've been spouting all day long? The gates and the sights and everything else. What happened to you?"

"What happened to me?"

He said it to himself, trembling. But he took control of his nerves and continued to speak to her quietly.

"They opened the border as soon as they completed the occupation, suddenly and immediately. That has never happened in any war in history. You know the terrible thing that happened in April 1948, so now, why this? Just for our sakes alone?[3] No! This is part of the war. They're saying to us, 'Help yourselves, look and see how much better we are than you, how much more developed. You should accept being our servants. You should admire us.' But you've seen it yourself. Nothing's changed. It was in our power to have done much better than they did."

"Then why did you come?"

He looked at her angrily and she fell silent.

She knew. Why did she need to ask? She was the one who told him to come. For twenty long years she avoided talking about it, twenty years. Then the past erupted as though forced out by a volcano.

As he drove the car through the center of Haifa, the smell of war was still strong enough to make the city seem to him dark and excited and agitated, the faces harsh and savage. After a little while he realized that he was driving the car through Haifa with the feeling that nothing in the streets had changed. He used to know Haifa stone by stone, intersection by intersection. How often he had crossed that road in his green 1946 Ford! Oh, he knew Haifa well, and now he felt as though he hadn't been away for twenty years. He was driving his car just as he used to, as though he hadn't been absent those twenty bitter years.

The names began to rain down inside his head as though a great layer of dust had been shaken off them: Wadi Nisnas, King Faisal Street, Hanatir Square, Halisa, Hadar[4] . . . The events mixed together suddenly, but he held himself together and asked his wife in a barely audible voice:

"Well, where shall we begin?"

She was quiet. He heard her crying softly, almost silently, and he calculated to himself the suffering she was enduring. He knew he couldn't really comprehend that suffering precisely, but he did know it was very great, and that it had remained so for twenty years. Now it was welling up like some incredible monster inside of her, in her head, in her heart, in her memories, in her imagination, controlling her entire future. He was amazed that he had never thought about what that suffering must have meant to her, and about the extent to which it was buried in the wrinkles of her face and in her eyes and in her mind. It was with her in every bite of food she took and in every hut where she had lived and in every look she cast at her children and at him and at herself. Now all of it was bursting forth from the wreckage and the oblivion and the pain, to carry away the mass of bitter defeat he had tasted at least twice in his lifetime.

All at once the past was upon him, sharp as a knife. He was turning his car at the end of King Faisal Street (for him, the street names had never changed) toward the intersection that descends left to the port and right to the road leading to Wadi Nisnas when he saw a group of armed soldiers standing in front of an iron barricade at the intersection. As he watched them out of the corner of his eye, a sound like an explosion burst out from the distance. Then a crack of gunfire, and the steering wheel began to tremble between his hands. He nearly ran up onto the sidewalk, but at the last moment he recovered himself and saw a young boy dashing across the road. With that scene the terrible past came back to him in all its tumultuousness. For the first time in twenty years he remembered what happened in minute detail, as though he were reliving it again.

Morning, Wednesday, April 21, 1948. Haifa, the city, was not expecting anything, in spite of the fact that it was filled with dark tension.

Thunder came abruptly from the east, from the heights of Mount Carmel. Mortar shells flew across the city's center, pelting the Arab quarters.

The streets of Haifa turned into chaos. Alarm swept through the city as it closed its shops and the windows of its houses.

Said S. was in the center of town when the sounds of shots and explosions started to fill the sky above Haifa. Up until noon he hadn't expected that this would be the all-out attack, so it wasn't until then that he tried to return home in his car, but he soon discovered that this was impossible. He went down the side streets in an attempt to cross the road to Halisa, where he lived, but the fighting had already spread, and he saw armed men racing from side street to main road and from main road to side street. They moved in obedience to instructions blaring from loudspeakers placed here and there. After a while Said felt he was rushing helter-skelter, yet the alleyways, closed off by machine guns or bullets or the soldiers themselves, seemed to be pushing him unconsciously in one direction only. Over and over as he tried to return to his real direction, picking out a particular alley, he found himself pushed by an unseen force toward one road only, the road to the coast.

He had married Safiyya a year and four months before and had rented a house in a neighborhood he figured would be safe. But now he felt he wouldn't reach it. He knew his young wife wouldn't be able to cope. Ever since he had brought her from the country she'd been unable to deal with city life or get used to all the complications which seemed to her terrifying and insoluble. What would happen to her now, he wondered?

He was lost, nearly. He didn't know exactly where or how the fighting was taking place. As far as he knew, the British still controlled the city and this whole situation should have taken place in approximately three weeks, when the British would begin to withdraw in accordance with the date they had fixed.

As he quickened his pace he knew for certain that he had to avoid the high sections of town adjoining Herzl Street, where the Jews had been headquartered from the beginning. But he also had to stay away from the business district between Halisa and Allenby Street, for that was the Jews' strongest arms base.

So he sped along trying to circle around the business district in order to reach Halisa. Before him was the road that ends at Wadi Nisnas and passes through the Old City.

All of a sudden things got mixed up and the names became tangled up in his head: Halisa, Wadi Rushmiyya, the Burj, the Old City, Wadi Nisnas.[5] He felt completely lost, that he had even lost his sense of direction. The explosions intensified. Even though he was far enough away from the site of the shooting he could still make out British soldiers who were boarding up some windows and opening others.

Somehow he found himself in the Old City and from there he raced with a strength he didn't know he possessed toward South Stanton Street. And then he knew he was less than two hundred meters away from Halul Street, and he began to catch the scent of the sea.

At that exact moment he remembered little Khaldun, his son who was five months old that very day, and a dark apprehension suddenly spread over him. It was the one taste that never left his tongue right up to this moment, twenty years after it happened for the first time.

Had he expected that disaster? The events were mixed up, the past and present running together, both in turn jumbled up with the thoughts and illusions and imaginings and feelings of twenty successive years. Had he known? Did he sense the calamity before it happened? Sometimes he told himself, "Yes, I knew it even before it happened." Other times he said, "No, I only imagined it after it happened. I couldn't possibly have expected anything as horrifying as that."

Evening began to settle over the city. He didn't know how many hours had passed as he rushed from street to street, but it was clear that he was being propelled toward the port. All the side streets leading off the main road were closed. He kept plunging down side streets trying to get to his house, but he was always driven back, sometimes by rifle muzzles, sometimes by bayonets.

The sky was on fire, crackling with shots, bombs and explosions, near and far. It was as though the very sounds themselves were pushing everyone toward the port. Even though he could not concentrate on anything specific, he couldn't help but see how the throng of people thickened with every step. People were pouring from the side streets into the main street leading down to the port—men, women and children, empty-handed or carrying a few small possessions, crying or being floated along in a paralyzed silence in the midst of the clamor and confusion. He was swallowed up in the rushing wave of humanity and lost the ability to direct his own steps. He kept remembering that he was being swept along by the dazed and crying throng toward the sea, unable to think about anything else. In his head was one picture only, suspended as though hanging on a wall: his wife Safiyya and his son Khaldun.

The moments passed slowly, relentlessly, making it seem like an incredibly severe nightmare. He went through the iron gate to the port where British soldiers were restraining people. From the gate he could see masses of people tumbling one over the other, falling into the small rowboats waiting near the wharf.[6] Without really knowing what he ought to do, he decided not to get into a rowboat. Then, like someone who suddenly goes insane or someone whose senses return all at once after a long period of insanity, he turned and began pushing through the throng with every ounce of strength he could muster, to forge a path through their midst, in the opposite direction, back toward the iron gate.

Like someone swimming against a torrent of water plummeting down a lofty mountain, Said forged ahead, using his shoulders and forearms, his thighs, even his head. The current carried him a few steps backward, but he pushed on wildly like some hunted creature hopelessly trying to forge a path through a thick tangle of undergrowth. Above him the smoke and the wailing of bombs and hail of gunfire fused with the screams, the footsteps, the sea's pounding, and the sound of oars slapping the surface of the waves . . .

Could twenty years really have passed since then?

Cold sweat poured down Said's forehead as he drove the car up the slope. He hadn't counted on the memory coming back full of the same insane turmoil that rightfully belonged only to the actual moments of the experience itself. He looked at his wife out of the corner of his eye. Her face was tense and pale, her eyes brimming with tears. Surely, he said to himself, she must be going back over her own steps that same day when he was as close as possible to the sea and she was as close as possible to the mountain, while between the two of them terror and destruction lengthened their unseen steps through the quagmire of screams and fear and uncertainty.

She had, so she had told him more than once over the past years, been thinking about him. When the shots rang out and people burst out with the news that the English and the Jews had begun to overrun Haifa, a desperate fear came over her.

She had been thinking about him when the sounds of war reached her from the center of town, for she knew he was there. She felt safe, so she remained in the house for a while. As his absence lengthened, she hurried out to the road without knowing exactly what she wanted to do there. At first she had looked out from the window, then from the balcony. Then she sensed that the situation had altered, for at noon fire began to pour down profusely from behind, from the hills above Halisa. She felt besieged all around, and only then did she dash down the steps and along the road toward the main street. The urgency of her desire to see him coming was a measure of her fear for him and her worry over the uncertain fate which carried a thousand possibilities with every shot fired. When she reached the top of the road, she quickly began to search the cars filing by, her steps guiding her from car to car and from person to person, asking questions without receiving a single answer. Suddenly she found herself in the middle of a wave of people pushing her as they themselves were being pushed from all over the city in a massive, unstoppable, powerful stream. She was carried along like a twig of straw.

How much time passed before she remembered that the infant Khaldun was still in his crib in Halisa?

She didn't remember exactly, but she knew that some staggering force rooted her to the ground, while the endless flow of people streamed by her and around her as though she were a tree surrounded by a flood of rushing water. She turned back, resisting the flood with all her strength. Weak and exhausted, she began to shout with all her might, but her words failed to rise above the ceaseless clamor to reach any ear. She repeated a thousand times, a million times, "Khaldun! Khaldun!" For months her injured voice remained hoarse, barely audible. That name, Khaldun, was the one unchanging note floating wretchedly in the midst of that endless torrent of voices and names.

She was on the verge of falling among the trampling feet when she heard, as though in a dream, a voice well up out of the ground, calling her name. When she saw his face behind her—dripping with sweat, rage, oppression—she was more horrified than ever. Sorrow pierced her, swept over her, filled her with boundless determination, and she resolved to return, no matter what the price. Perhaps she felt that she would never again be able to look Said in the eye, or let him touch her. In the depths of her soul she felt she was about to lose them both—Said and Khaldun. She forged her way through, using all the strength in her arms, through the jungle blocking her return, trying at the same time to lose Said, who was alternately calling, "Safiyya! Khaldun! . . ."

Did centuries pass, and destinies, before she felt his two strong, rigid hands fasten about her arms?

Then she looked into his eyes and, paralyzed, collapsed against his shoulder like a worthless scrap of cloth. Around them passed the flood of humanity, pushing them from side to side, forcing them along toward the shore, but beyond that they were incapable of feeling anything at all until they were splashed by spray flying up from the oars and they looked back toward shore to see Haifa clouding over behind the evening's dusk and the twilight of their tears . . .

2✤ All the way from Ramallah to Jerusalem to Haifa he talked about everything, without stopping for a moment. But when he reached the entrance to Bat Gallim,[7] silence bound his tongue. Here he was in Halisa, listening to the sound his car wheels always made when they turned. The furious beating of his agitated heart made him lose himself from time to time. Twenty years of absence had dwindled away and suddenly, incredibly, things were right back to where they had been, despite all reason and logic. What could he be looking for?

A week ago, in their house in Ramallah, Safiyya had said to him:

"They're going everywhere now. Why don't we go to Haifa?"

He was having dinner at the time. He saw his hand stop involuntarily between the plate and his mouth. He looked at her after a moment and saw her turn away so he wouldn't be able to read anything in her eyes. Then he said to her:

"Go to Haifa? Why?"

Her voice was soft:

"To see our house. Just to see it."

He placed the bite of food back on his plate, got up and stood in front of her. She held her head low against her chest like someone confessing to an unexpected sin. He placed his fingers under her chin and raised her head to look into her eyes, which were moist with tears. Compassionately, he asked her:

"Safiyya, what are you thinking about?"

She nodded her head in agreement without speaking, for she knew that he knew. Perhaps he too was thinking about it all along but was waiting for her to bring it up, so she wouldn't feel—as she always did—as though she had been the one at fault for the catastrophe that had occurred in both of their hearts. He whispered hoarsely:

"Khaldun?"

All at once that name which had remained unspoken for so many years was out in the open. The few times they had spoken of the child they always said "him." They avoided giving any of their other three sons that name, although they called the eldest Khalid and the daughter who followed a year and a half later,

Khalida. Said himself was called Abu Khalid,[8] and old friends who knew what happened all agreed to say that Khaldun had died. How could the past come rushing in now by the back door in such an extraordinary way?

Said remained standing as though asleep some place far away. After a while he came to himself and strode back to his place. Before he sat down he said:

"Delusions, Safiyya, delusions! Don't deceive yourself so tragically. You know how we questioned and investigated. You know the stories of the Red Cross and the peace-keeping forces, and the foreign friends we sent there. No, I don't want to go to Haifa. It's a disgrace. If it's a disgrace for the people of Haifa, for you and me it's a double disgrace. Why torture ourselves?"

Her sobbing grew louder, but she didn't say anything. They passed the night without a word, listening to the sound of soldiers' boots striking the road and to the radio still giving the news.

When he went to bed he knew in his heart that there was no escape. The thought lurking there for twenty years had finally come to light and there was no way to bury it again. Even though he knew that his wife wasn't asleep, that she, too, was thinking about the same thing all night long, he didn't speak to her. In the morning she said to him quietly:

"If you want to go, take me with you. Said, don't try to go alone."

He knew Safiyya well, he knew the way she could sense every thought that went through his mind. Once again she had stopped him in his tracks. During the night he had decided to go alone, and here she had uncovered his decision instinctively and forbidden it.

It remained hanging over them, day and night, for a week. They ate it with their food and slept with it, but they did not speak a word about it. Then, just last night, he said to her:

"Let's go to Haifa tomorrow. At least take a look. Maybe we can pass near our house. I think they're going to issue an order prohibiting it soon. Their calculations were wrong."

He was quiet for a moment. He wasn't sure whether he wanted to change the subject, but he heard himself continue:

"In Jerusalem and Nablus and here people talk every day

about their visits to Jaffa, Acre, Tel Aviv, Haifa, Safad, towns in Galilee and in Muthallath.[9] They all tell the same story. It seems that what they saw with their own eyes didn't measure up to their speculations. Most of them bring back stories of failure. Apparently, the miracle the Jews talked about was nothing but an illusion. There's a strong negative reaction in this country, exactly the opposite of what they wanted when they opened their border to us. That's why, Safiyya, I expect them to rescind the order soon. So I said to myself, why don't we take advantage of the opportunity and go?"

When he looked at Safiyya, she was trembling, and he saw her face become deathly pale as she fled from the room. He himself felt burning tears block his throat. From that point on the name Khaldun had not stopped ringing in his head, exactly as it had twenty years ago, over and over above the surging throng at the port. It had to be the same for Safiyya because they talked about everything throughout the trip, everything except Khaldun. Finally, nearing Bat Gallim, they fell silent. Here they were, gazing silently at the road they both knew so well, its memory stuck fast in their heads like part of their very flesh and bones.

As he used to do twenty years before, he slowed the car down to its lowest gear before reaching the curve that he knew concealed a difficult rocky surface behind it. He turned the car the way he always did and climbed the slope, watching out for the exact spot on the narrowing road. The three cypress trees that hung over the road had new branches. He wanted to stop a moment to read the names carved long ago on their trunks; he could almost remember them one by one. But he didn't stop. He didn't remember exactly how things had happened, but it started to come back to him when he passed a door he knew, where someone from the priest's family used to live. The priest's family owned a large building on South Stanton Street, near Halul Street. It was in that building—the day of the flight—that the Arab fighters barricaded themselves and fought to their last bullet and maybe their last man. He had passed that building when he was pushed toward the port by a force that surpassed his own strength. He remembered exactly that it was there and only there when the memory fell upon him like a blow from a rock. There, exactly, he had remembered Khaldun, and his heart had pounded that day twenty years ago and it continued pounding harder still today until it was nearly loud enough to be heard.

Suddenly, the house loomed up, the very house he had first lived in, then kept alive in his memory for so long. Here it was again, its front balcony bearing its coat of yellow paint.

Instantly he imagined that Safiyya, young again with her hair in a long braid, was about to lean over the balcony toward him. There was a new clothesline attached to two pegs on the balcony; new bits of washing, red and white, hung on the line. Safiyya began to cry audibly. He turned to the right and direct-ed the car's wheels up over the low curb, then stopped the car in its old spot. Just like he used to do—exactly—twenty years ago.

Said S. hesitated for just a moment as he let the engine die down. But he knew inside himself that if he hesitated for very long, it would end right there. He would start up the engine again and leave. So he made the whole thing appear, to himself and to his wife, perfectly natural, as though the past twenty years had been put between two huge presses and crushed until they became a thin piece of transparent paper. He got out of the car and slammed the door behind him. He hitched up his belt and looked toward the balcony, absently jingling the keys in his palm.

Safiyya came around the car to his side, but she was not as composed as he was. He took her by the arm and crossed the street with her—the sidewalk, the green iron gate, the stairs.

They began to climb, and he didn't give either of them the opportunity to see all the little things that would jolt and throw them off balance—the bell and the copper lock and the bullet holes in the wall and the electricity box and the fourth step bro-ken in its center and the smooth carved balustrade which the palm slid over and the unyielding iron grillwork of the *masa-tib*[10] and the first floor, where Mahjub es-Saadi lived, where the door was always ajar and the children always playing in front, filling the stairway with their shouts—past all of that and on to the recently painted wooden door, firmly closed.

He put his fingers on the bell and said to Safiyya quietly:
"They changed the bell."

He was silent a moment, then added:

"And the name. Naturally."

He forced a foolish smile onto his face and placed his hand
over Safiyya's. Her hand was cold and trembling. From behind
the door they heard slow footsteps. "An elderly person, no
doubt," he said to himself. There was the muffled sound of a
bolt creaking, and the door opened slowly.

"So this is she." He didn't know whether he said it out loud
or to himself in the form of a deep sigh. He remained standing
in the same place without knowing what he should do. He chid-
ed himself for not having prepared an opening sentence in spite
of the fact that he had known with certainty that this very
moment would arrive. He stirred himself and looked toward
Safiyya for help. Umm Khalid[11] thereupon took a step forward
and said:

"May we come in?"

The old woman didn't understand. She was short and
rather plump and was dressed in a blue dress with white polka
dots. As Said began to translate into English, the lines of her
face came together, questioning. She stepped aside, allowing
Said and Safiyya to enter, then led them into the living room.

Said followed her, Safiyya at his side, with slow, hesitant
steps. They began to pick out the things around them with a
certain bewilderment. The entrance seemed smaller than he
had imagined it and felt a little damp. He saw many things he
had once considered—and for that matter still considered—to
be intimate and personal, things he believed were sacred and
private property which no one had the right to become familiar
with, to touch, or even to look at. A photograph of Jerusalem he
remembered very clearly still hung where it had when he lived
there. On the opposite wall a small Syrian carpet also remained
where it had always hung.

He looked around, rediscovering the items, sometimes little
by little and sometimes all at once, like someone recovering
from a long period of unconsciousness. When they reached the
living room he saw two chairs from the set of five he used to

own. The other three chairs were new, and they seemed crude and out of harmony with the rest of the furnishings. In the center of the room was the same inlaid table, although its color had faded a bit. The glass vase on top of the table had been replaced by a wooden one, and in it was a bunch of peacock feathers. He knew there used to be seven of them. He tried to count them from where he was sitting, but he couldn't, so he got up, moved closer to the vase and counted them one by one. There were only five.

When he turned to go back to his seat, he saw that the curtains were different. The ones Safiyya had made twenty years ago from sugar-colored yarn had been taken down and replaced by curtains with long blue threads running through them.

Then his gaze fell on Safiyya and he saw that she seemed confused. She was examining the corners of the room as though counting up the things that were missing. The old woman was sitting in front of them on the arm of one of the chairs, looking at them with a blank smile on her face. Finally, without changing her smile, she said:

"I have been expecting you for a long time."

Her English was hesitant and marked by something like a German accent. She seemed to be pulling the words up out of a bottomless well as she pronounced them.

Said leaned forward and asked her:

"Do you know who we are?"

She nodded several times to emphasize her certainty. She thought for a moment, choosing her words, then said slowly:

"You are the owners of this house. I know that."

"How do you know?"

Said and Safiyya both asked the question simultaneously.

The old woman continued to smile. Then she said:

"From everything. From the photographs, from the way the two of you stood in front of the door. The truth is, ever since the war ended many people have come here, looking at the houses and going into them. Every day I said that surely you would come."

At once she seemed to become confused and began to look around at the things distributed throughout the room as though she were seeing them for the first time. Involuntarily, Said followed her glance, moving his eyes from place to place as she moved hers. Safiyya did the same. He said to himself, "How strange! Three pairs of eyes looking at one thing . . . but how differently each see it!"

The old woman spoke then, more quietly now and even more slowly.

"I'm sorry. But that's what happened. I never thought things would be the way they are now."

Said smiled bitterly. He didn't know how he could say to her that he hadn't come for that, that he wouldn't get into a political discussion, that he knew she wasn't guilty of anything.

She, not guilty of anything?

No, not exactly. But how could he explain it to her?

Safiyya saved him the trouble for she began to question the woman in a voice that seemed suspiciously innocent. Said translated.

"Where did you come from?"

"From Poland."

"When?"

"1948."

"When exactly?"

"March 1st, 1948."

A heavy silence prevailed. All of them began to look around at things they had no need to look at. Said broke the silence, saying calmly:

"Naturally we didn't come to tell you to get out of here. That would take a war . . ."

Safiyya pressed his hand to keep him from veering away from the conversation, and he understood. He continued, trying to keep his words closer to the subject.

"I mean, your presence here, in this house, our house, Safiyya's and my house, is another matter. We only came to take a look at things, our things. Maybe you can understand that."

She said quickly:

"I understand, but . . ."

Then he lost his composure. "Yes, but! This terrible, deadly, enduring 'but' . . ."

He fell silent beneath the pressure of his wife's gaze. He felt he'd never be able to reach his goal. They were on a collision course here, it couldn't be denied. What was going on now was nothing more than absurd talk.

For a moment he wanted to get up and leave. Nothing mattered to him anymore. Whether Khaldun was alive or dead made no difference. How things reached that point he simply couldn't say. He was filled with helpless, bitter anger and felt as if he were about to explode inside. He didn't know how his gaze happened to fall upon the five peacock feathers stuck in the wooden vase in the middle of the room. He saw their rare, beautiful colors shifting in the puffs of wind coming from the open window. Pointing at the vase, he demanded gruffly:

"There were seven feathers. What happened to the two missing feathers?"

The old woman looked where he was pointing, then looked at him again questioningly. He continued to hold his arm outstretched toward the vase, staring, demanding an answer. His entire universe hung in the balance, poised on the tip of her tongue. She rose from her chair and grasped the vase as though for the first time. Slowly she said:

"I don't know where the two feathers you speak of went. I can't remember. Maybe Dov played with them when he was a child and lost them."

"Dov?"

They said it together, Said and Safiyya. They stood up as if the earth had flung them up. They looked at her tensely, and she continued:

"Of course. Dov. I don't know what his name used to be, nor if it even matters to you, but he looks a lot like you . . ."

3 ❧ Now, after two hours of intermittent talk, it was possible to put things back in order, that is, to sort out what had happened in those few days between Wednesday night, April 21, 1948, when Said S. left Haifa on a British boat, pushed aboard with his wife, to be cast off an hour later on the empty shore of Acre, and Thursday, April 29, 1948, when a member of the Haganah,[12] accompanied by a man who looked like a chicken, opened the door of Said S.'s house in Halisa. With that opening, the way was cleared for Iphrat Koshen and his wife, who had both come from Poland, to enter what from then on became their house, rented from the Bureau of Absentee Property in Haifa.[13]

Iphrat Koshen reached Haifa via Milan early in the month of March under the auspices of the Jewish Agency.[14] He had left Warsaw with a small convoy of people in early November of 1947. He lived in a temporary residence on the outskirts of the Italian port, which at the time was fraught with unaccustomed activity. At the beginning of March he was transferred by ship with some of the other men and women to Haifa.

His papers were in perfect order. A small truck carried him and his few possessions across the clamorous port area, which was filled with merchandise and teeming with British soldiers and Arab workers, and on through the tense streets of Haifa that rumbled with sporadic gunfire. At Hadar he lived in a small room in a building choked with people.

Iphrat Koshen soon realized that most of the rooms in the building were packed with new emigres waiting for eventual transfer to some other place. He didn't know whether the residents themselves came up with the name "Emigres' Lodge" as they sat together eating dinner each night or whether it had been known by that name before and they were merely making use of it.

Perhaps he had looked out at Halisa from his balcony a few times, but he didn't know or couldn't even guess that he would come to live there. In truth, he believed that when things calmed down he'd go to live in a quiet house in the country at the foot of some hill in Galilee. He'd read *Thieves in the Night* by Arthur Koestler[15] while in Milan; a man who came from England to oversee the emigration operation had lent it to him. This man had lived for a while on the very hill in Galilee that Koestler used as the background for his novel. Actually, not much was known about Palestine at that time. For Iphrat,

Palestine was nothing more than a stage set adapted from an old legend and still decorated in the manner of the colorful scenes pictured in Christian religious books designed to be used by children in Europe. Of course, he didn't fully believe that the land was only a desert rediscovered by the Jewish Agency after two thousand years,[16] but that wasn't what mattered most to him then. He'd been placed in a residence where something called "waiting" caused him to be taken up with daily concerns like the others there with him.

Perhaps because he'd heard gunfire ever since leaving the port of Haifa at the end of that first week of March 1948, he didn't think very much about whether something terrible might be happening at the time. In any event, he had never met a single Arab in his entire life. In fact, it was in Haifa that he came upon his first Arab, a year and a half after the occupation. The whole situation was such that he could keep a picture in his mind throughout those oppressive days, a picture that was concealed and isolated from what was really happening. It was a mythical picture, in perfect harmony with what he had imagined in Warsaw or in Milan during the twenty-five years of his life. So the fighting he heard and read about every morning in the *Palestine Post* seemed to be taking place between men and ghosts, nothing more.

Where, exactly, was he on Wednesday, April 21, 1948, at the time when Said S. was lost between Allenby Street and Halul, and Safiyya was rushing from Halisa down to the edge of the business district in the direction of Stanton Street?

It was impossible to remember the events precisely and in detail at this point. However, he remembered that the battle that began Wednesday morning lasted continuously until Thursday evening. Only on Friday morning, April 23, could he tell for sure that it was all over in Haifa; the Haganah controlled the entire area. He really didn't know exactly what had happened. The explosions seemed to come from Hadar, and the details gathered from the radio and from news brought by people coming in from time to time melded together in such a way as to make it all too difficult to understand. But he knew that the decisive attack that had begun on Wednesday morning had been launched from three centers and that Colonel Moshe Karmatil[17] was directing three battalions in Hadar Ha-Carmel and the business district. One of the battalions was to sweep through Halisa, the bridge and Wadi Rushmiyya, toward the port. At the same time, another battalion was to press forward from the business district in order to block off the people who were fleeing by forcing them along a narrow street that led to the sea.[18] Iphrat didn't know the precise locations of the positions whose names he remembered from sheer repetition, but there was a connection between the words *Irgun*[19] and *Wadi Nisnas* that led him to understand that the Irgun was in charge of the attack from that location.

Iphrat Koshen didn't need anyone to tell him that the English had an interest in delivering Haifa into the hands of the Haganah. It was well within his knowledge that they had played, and continued to play, a joint role. He'd seen it for himself two or three times. He didn't remember how he came by the information about the role of Brigadier Stockwell,[20] but he was sure it was true. The rumor was circulating in every corner of the Emigres' Lodge that Brigadier Stockwell threw his weight to the Haganah. He concealed the date of the British withdrawal and leaked it only to the Haganah, thereby giving them the element of surprise at the most appropriate moment, when the Arabs were figuring that the British Army would relinquish its power at a later date.[21]

Iphrat stayed at the Emigres' Lodge all that Wednesday and Thursday, for they had been instructed not to leave the building. Some began to go out on Friday, but he didn't go out until Saturday morning. He was immediately struck by the fact that he didn't see any cars. It was a true Jewish Sabbath! This brought tears to his eyes for reasons he couldn't explain. When his wife saw this, she too was surprised and said to him with tears in her own eyes:

"I'm crying for another reason. Yes, this is a true Sabbath. But there is no longer a true Sabbath on Friday, nor a true one on Sunday."[22]

That was just the beginning. For the first time since his arrival, his wife had called his attention to something troubling, something which he had neither counted on nor thought about. The signs of destruction that he began to notice took on another meaning, but he refused to let himself worry or even think about it.

From the standpoint of his wife Miriam, however, the situation was different. It changed that very day as she passed near Bethlehem Church in Hadar. She saw two young men from the Haganah carrying something, which they put in a small truck stopped nearby. In a flash she saw what it was they were carrying. She grabbed her husband's arm and, trembling, cried out:

"Look!"

But her husband didn't see anything when he looked where she was pointing. The two men were wiping their palms on the sides of their khaki shirts. She said to her husband: "That was a dead Arab child! I saw it! And it was covered with blood!"

Her husband guided her across the street, then asked:

"How do you know it was an Arab child?"

"Didn't you see how they threw it onto the truck, like a piece of wood? If it had been a Jewish child they would never have done that."

He wanted to ask her why, but when he saw her face, he remained silent.

Miriam had lost her father at Auschwitz eight years before. When they raided the house where she lived with her husband, he wasn't home, so she took refuge with the upstairs neighbors. The German soldiers didn't find anyone, but on their way back down the stairs they came upon her ten-year-old brother, who most likely had been on his way to tell her that their father had been sent to the camps, leaving him all alone. When he saw the German soldiers, he turned and began running away. She saw it all through the narrow slit made by a short gap between the stairs. She also saw how they shot him down.

By the time Iphrat and Miriam got back to the Emigres' Lodge, Miriam had decided to return to Italy. But she couldn't, either that night or in the next few days, convince her husband. She always lost the arguments quickly and couldn't find the words to express her views or explain the real meaning of her motives.

A week later, however, the situation changed again. Her

husband returned from a trip to the office of the Jewish Agency in Haifa with two bits of good news: they had been given a house right in Haifa, and along with the house, a five-month-old baby!

Thursday evening, April 22, 1948. Tura Zonshtein, the divorced woman who lived with her small son on the third floor, right above Said S., heard a sound coming from the second floor of a baby weakly crying.

At first, she could not believe the immediate thought that came into her mind. But when the whimpering continued, she roused herself and went down to the second floor and knocked on the door.

Finally, she felt compelled to break the door open. There was the child in his crib, completely exhausted. She carried him up to her own house.

Tura figured that things would return to normal soon. It didn't take long, however—only two or three days—before that assessment fell apart. She realized that the situation was completely different from what she had figured it to be. It wasn't possible for her to continue to look after the baby, so she took him to the office of the Jewish Agency in Haifa where she thought something would be done to solve the problem.

It was Iphrat Koshen's luck to come in to that office a few minutes later. When the officials saw from his papers that he didn't have any children, they offered him a house right in Haifa as a special concession if he agreed to adopt the child.

This proposition came as a complete surprise to Iphrat, who had been longing to adopt a child ever since he'd learned for certain that Miriam couldn't have children. The whole thing seemed to him to be a gift from God; he could hardly believe it had come about so suddenly, just like that. Without a doubt, a child would change Miriam completely and put a stop to the strange ideas that had been filling her mind continuously ever since she'd seen the dead Arab child thrown onto the death cart like a lump of worthless wood.

Thus the day was Thursday, the 29th[23] of April, 1948, the day when Iphrat Koshen and his wife Miriam, accompanied by the chicken-faced man from the Jewish Agency carrying a five-month-old baby, entered the house of Said S. in Halisa.

As for Said and Safiyya, on that same day they were weeping together after Said had returned from the last of his endless attempts to get back into Haifa. Racked and overcome, he slept from sheer exhaustion, as though unconscious. This was in a sixth-grade classroom in a secondary school, facing one of the walls surrounding the notorious Acre prison on the western seashore.[24]

Said didn't touch Miriam's coffee. Safiyya took just one sip, and with it a piece of one of the tinned biscuits Miriam had smilingly put before them.

Said continued to look around. His confusion had lessened somewhat as he listened to Miriam's story unfold little by little during what seemed a very long time. He and Safiyya remained nailed to their chairs, waiting for something unknown to take place, something they couldn't imagine.

Miriam came and went, and each time she disappeared behind the door, they listened to her slow steps dragging along the floor tiles. If she closed her eyes, Safiyya could imagine exactly Miriam going down the hall leading to the kitchen. On the right was the bedroom. Once, when they heard a door slam, Safiyya looked at Said and said bitterly:

"As if she's in her own house! She acts as if it's her house!"

They smiled in silence. Said pressed his palms together between his knees, unable to decide what to do. Finally, Miriam returned and they asked her:

"When will he get here?"

"It's time for him to return now, but he's late. He never was on time getting home. He's just like his father. He was . . ."

She broke off. Biting her lip, she looked at Said, who was trembling as if he'd been hit by an electric shock. "Like his father!" Then suddenly he asked himself, "What is fatherhood?" It was like throwing a window wide open to an unexpected cyclone. He put his head between his hands to try to stop the wild spinning of the question that had been suppressed somewhere in his mind for twenty years, the question he'd never dared to face. Safiyya began to stroke his shoulder, for in some uncanny way she understood what he felt, the sudden impact of words colliding to bring about the inevitable. She said:

"Look who's talking! She said, 'Like his father!' As if Khaldun had a father other than you!"

But then Miriam stepped forward and stood preparing herself to say something difficult. Slowly she began to extract the words, and it seemed as though unseen hands were pulling them from the depths of a well full of dust.

"Listen, Mr. Said. I want to tell you something important. I wanted you to wait for Dov—or Khaldun, if you like—so you could talk to each other and the matter could end as it naturally should end. Do you think this hasn't been as much of a problem for me as it's been for you? For the past twenty years I've been confused, but now the time has come for us to finish the matter. I know who his father is. And I also know that he is our son. But let's call on him to decide. Let's call on him to choose. He's of age and we must recognize that he's the only one who has the right to choose. Do you agree?"

Said got up and walked around the room. He stopped in front of the inlaid table and once more began to count the feathers in the wooden vase perched there. He said nothing. He kept silent as though he had not heard a word. Miriam watched him expectantly. Finally, he turned to Safiyya and told her what Miriam had said. Safiyya got up and stood by his side and said, her voice trembling:

"That's a fair choice. I'm certain Khaldun will choose his real parents. It's impossible to deny the call of flesh and blood."

Said burst out laughing, his laughter filled with a profound bitterness that bespoke defeat.

"What Khaldun, Safiyya? What Khaldun? What flesh and blood are you talking about? You say this is a fair choice? They've taught him how to be for twenty years, day by day, hour by hour, with his food, his drink, his sleep. And you say, a fair choice! Truly Khaldun, or Dov, or the devil if you like, doesn't know us! Do you want to know what I think? Let's get out of here and return to the past. The matter is finished. They stole him."

He looked over at Safiyya, who had collapsed into her chair.

All at once, for the first time, she faced the truth. Said's words seemed to her to be true, but she was still trying to hang on to the invisible thread of hope she had constructed in her imagination for twenty years as a sort of bribe. Her husband said to her:

"Maybe he never knew at all that he was born of Arab parents. Or maybe he learned it a month ago, a week ago, a year ago. What do you think? He was deceived, and perhaps he was even more enthusiastic in the deception than they were. The crime began twenty years ago and there's no doubt who paid the price. It began the day we left him here."

"But we didn't leave him. You know that."

"Yes, sure. We shouldn't have left anything. Not Khaldun, not the house, not Haifa! Didn't the same frightening feeling come over you that came over me while I was driving through the streets of Haifa? I felt as though I knew Haifa, yet the city refused to acknowledge me. I had the same feeling in this house, here, in our house. Can you imagine that? That our house would refuse to acknowledge us? Don't you feel it? I believe the same thing will happen with Khaldun. You'll see!"

Safiyya began to sob miserably. Miriam left the room, which now seemed filled with a palpable tension. Said felt as if all the walls he'd made himself live inside of for twenty years had shattered, letting him see things clearly. He waited until Safiyya's sobbing subsided, then turned to her and asked:

"Do you know what happened to Faris al-Lubda?"

"Ibn al-Lubda?[25] Our neighbor?"

"Of course. Our neighbor in Ramallah who went to Kuwait. Do you know what happened to him when he visited his house in Jaffa just a week ago?"

"He went to Jaffa?"

"Of course. A week ago I think. He hired a car from Jerusalem. He went straight to the Ajami quarter. Twenty years ago he lived in a two-story house behind the Orthodox school in Ajami. Remember the school? It's behind the Freres school,[26] heading left, toward Jabaliyya, after about two hundred meters the Orthodox school is on the right. It's got a large playground. There's an alley just beyond the playground. Faris al-Lubda lived in the middle of that alley with his family. His anger was boiling that day. He told the driver to stop in front of the house. He took the stairs two at a time and knocked on the door of his house."

4 ❧ It was afternoon. Except for the Manshiyya quarter,[27] Jaffa was still the same as when Faris al-Lubda knew it twenty years earlier. The few seconds that elapsed between the time he knocked on the door and the time he heard the approaching footsteps of the man who would open it lengthened into an eternity of anger and helpless, paralyzed sorrow. Finally, the door opened. The man was tall and brown-skinned and wore a white shirt with the buttons open. He stretched out his hand to greet the newcomer. Faris ignored the outstretched hand and spoke with controlled anger.

"I came to have a look at my house. This place where you are living is my house. Your presence here is a sorry comedy that will end one day by the power of the sword. If you wish, you can shoot me right here on the spot, but this is still my house. I've waited twenty years to return. And if . . ."

The man standing on the threshold continued to hold out his hand. He laughed heartily, coming closer to Faris until he was directly in front of him. Then he offered his two open arms and embraced him.

"You don't need to vent your anger on me. I am also an Arab, from Jaffa, like you. I know you. You're Ibn al-Lubda. Come in and have some coffee!"

Baffled, Faris entered. He could hardly believe it. It was the same house, the same furniture and arrangement, the same color on the walls, and all the things he remembered so well. Still smiling broadly, the man led him toward the living room. When he opened the living room door and invited him to enter, Faris stopped, nailed to the floor. His eyes welled up.

The living room was exactly as if he'd left it that morning. It was filled with the same smell as before, the smell of the sea, which always used to stir up a maelstrom in his head of unknown worlds ready to invade and challenge. But that wasn't what rooted him to his spot. On the glossy white wall facing him a picture of his brother Badr was still hanging, the only picture in the entire room. The wide black ribbon that stretched across the corner of the picture was still there too.

An air of mourning suddenly flooded the room, and tears began to roll down Faris's cheeks as he stood there. Those days were long ago, but now they burst forth as though the portals that had held them back were thrown wide open.

His brother Badr was the first one in Ajami to carry arms that first week of December 1947. From that point on, the house was transformed into a meeting place for the young men who used to fill the playground of the Orthodox school every afternoon. Badr joined the fighting as though he'd been waiting for that day since childhood. Then, on April 6, 1948, Badr was carried home on his companions' shoulders. His pistol was still at his waist, but his rifle, like his body, had been smashed by the grenade that struck him on the road to Tall al-Rish.[28] Ajami escorted his body in a funeral procession befitting a martyr. One of his companions took an enlarged picture of Badr to Iskandar Iwad Street where a calligrapher named Qutub wrote out a small placard saying that Badr al-Lubda was martyred for the sake of his country's independence. One child carried the placard at the head of the funeral procession, while two other children carried Badr's picture. In the evening the picture was returned to the house and a black mourning ribbon was tied to the right-hand corner.

He still remembered how his mother took down all the other pictures hanging on the living room wall and hung Badr's picture on the wall facing the door. From then on the sad smell of mourning permeated the room, and people kept coming to sit there, look at the picture, and offer their sympathy.

From where he stood, Faris could still see the nail heads, which had held other pictures twenty years before, protruding from the naked walls. They looked like men standing and waiting in front of that large picture of his martyred brother, Badr al-Lubda, hanging by itself, draped in black, in the heart of the room.

The man said to Faris:

"Come in, sit down. We need to talk a little. We've been waiting for you[29] a long time, but we hoped to see you under different circumstances."

Faris entered as if he were walking across some incredible dream. He sat in a chair facing his brother's picture. It was the first time he'd seen it in twenty years. When they left Jaffa (a boat carried them from Shatt al-Shabab[30] toward Gaza, but his father returned and went to Jordan), they didn't take anything with them, not even the picture of Badr that remained there.

Faris couldn't utter a sound. Then two children came into the room, ran about between the chairs, and left, shouting as they had come. The man said:

"They are Saad and Badr, my sons."

"Badr?"

"Of course, we gave him the name of your martyred brother."

"And the picture?"

The man stopped, his face changed. Then he said:

"I'm from Jaffa, a resident of Manshiyya. In the 1948 War a mortar shell destroyed my house. I don't want to go into how Jaffa fell and how the ones who came to help us withdrew at the critical moment.[31] That's all over now. The important thing is, when I returned with the fighters to the abandoned city they arrested us, and I was in a prison camp for a long time. When they let me go I refused to leave Jaffa. I happened upon this house and rented it from the government."

"And the picture?"

"When I came to the house, the picture was the first thing I saw. Maybe I rented the house because of it. It's complicated and I can't really explain it to you. When they occupied Jaffa it was a deserted city. After I got out of jail, I felt as if I were under siege. I didn't see a single Arab here. I was a tiny island, alone and isolated in a sea of raging hostility. You didn't experience that agony, but I lived it.

"When I saw the picture, I found consolation in it, a companion that spoke to me, to remind me of things I could be proud of, things I considered to be the best in our lives. So I decided to rent the house. At that time, like now, it seemed to me that for a man to have a companion who bears arms and dies for his country is something precious that can't be tossed aside. Maybe it was a kind of loyalty to those who fought. I felt that getting rid of it would be an unforgivable betrayal. It helped me not just to resist but also to remain. That's why the picture stayed here. It remained a part of our lives. Me, my wife Lamia, my son Badr, my son Saad, your brother Badr—we're all one family. We've lived together for twenty years. This was something very important to us."

Faris sat there until midnight looking at his brother Badr, full of youth and vigor beneath that black sash, smiling in the picture just as he had for twenty years. When Faris got up to leave, he asked if he could take the picture. The man said:

"Of course. He's your brother, above and beyond anything else."

He got up and took the picture down from the wall. Behind it remained a pale, meaningless rectangle, a disturbing void.

Faris carried the picture out to the car and set off again for Ramallah. All the way home he kept looking at it, lying on the seat beside him. Badr looked out from the picture, smiling that smile of awakening youth. Faris remained like this until they crossed Jerusalem and were on the road for Ramallah. Then suddenly the feeling came over him that he had no right to keep the picture, although he couldn't explain why. He ordered the driver to return to Jaffa and got there in the morning.

He climbed the stairs again, slowly, and knocked at the door. As he took the picture from Faris, the man said:

"I felt a terrible emptiness when I looked at the rectangle left behind on the wall. My wife cried and my children got very upset. I regretted letting you take the picture. In the end, this man is one of us. We lived with him and he lived with us and became part of us. During the night I said to my wife that if you[32] wanted to reclaim him, you'd have to reclaim the house, Jaffa, us . . . The picture doesn't solve your problem, but with respect to us, it's your bridge to us and our bridge to you."

Faris returned to Ramallah alone. Said S. said to his wife:

"Faris al-Lubda, if you only knew . . ."

He whispered in a barely audible voice:

"Now he's carrying arms."

5

On the street a motor rumbled. Miriam came into the room, her face turning pale. It was nearly midnight. The old woman went over to the window and drew back the curtain gently, then announced in a trembling voice:

"Here's Dov. He's come!"

The footsteps on the stairs sounded youthful but tired. Said S. followed them one after another as they climbed the stairs. He listened with nerves taut from the moment he heard the iron gate slam and the bolt lock.

The minutes lengthened, their silence fairly clamoring with a crazy, unbearable ringing. Then came the sound of a key fumbling at the door. Only then did Said look toward Miriam and realize for the first time that she was sitting there trembling, her face pale. He didn't have enough courage to look at Safiyya, so he fastened his eyes on the door, feeling the sweat drip from every pore of his body.

The footsteps in the hallway were muffled and seemed confused. Then came a half-raised voice, hesitant:

"Mama?"

Miriam shuddered slightly and rubbed her hands together. Said listened to Safiyya quietly choking back tears. The footsteps hesitated a little, as if waiting for something. Again the same voice spoke, and when it fell silent, Miriam translated in a trembling whisper:

"He's asking why I'm in the living room at this late hour."

The footsteps continued heading toward the room. The door was ajar, and Miriam said in English:

"Come here, Dov. There are some guests who wish to see you."

The door opened slowly. At first it was hard to believe, since the light by the door was dim, but then the tall man stepped forward: he was wearing a military uniform and carrying his military cap in his hand.

Said leaped to his feet as though an electric current had flung him out of his chair. He looked at Miriam and said tensely:

"Is this the surprise? Is this the surprise you wanted us to wait for?"

Safiyya turned away toward the window and hid her face in her hands, sobbing openly.

The young man remained by the door, shifting his gaze among the three of them, confused. Miriam stood up and said to him slowly, with artificial calmness:

"I would like to present to you your parents—your original parents."

Slowly he took a step forward. His face changed color and it seemed as if he had lost his self-confidence all at once. He looked down at his uniform, then back at Said, who was still standing in front of him, staring at him. Finally he said, in a subdued voice:

"I don't know any mother but you. As for my father, he was killed in the Sinai eleven years ago.[33] I know no others than the two of you."

Said took two steps back, sat down, and placed Safiyya's hand between his own. He was inwardly amazed at how quickly he was able to regain his composure. If anyone had told him five minutes earlier that he'd be sitting there so calmly now, he would not have believed it. But everything was different now.

Slowly the minutes passed, while everything remained motionless. Then the young man began to pace slowly: three steps toward the middle of the room, three steps toward the door, then back to the middle of the room. He set his cap on the table, and somehow it seemed inappropriate, almost laughable, next to the wooden vase full of peacock feathers. The strange sensation came over Said that he was watching a play prepared ahead of time in detail. It reminded him of cheap melodramas in trivial movies with artificial plots.

The young man approached Miriam and said to her in a voice meant to be decisive, final, and to be heeded implicitly:

"What did the two of them come for? Don't tell me they want to take me back?"

In a similar manner, Miriam replied:

"Ask them."

He turned stiffly, as if following an order, and asked Said:

"What do you want, sir?"

Said held his composure, which seemed to him to be nothing more than a thin shell barely covering a smoldering flame. His voice muffled, he said:

"Nothing. Nothing, just . . . curiosity, you know."

A sudden silence fell, and through it rose the sounds of Safiyya's sobs, rather like the creaking chair of an uninvolved observer. The young man shifted his gaze again from Said to Miriam, then to his cap lying against the wooden vase. He retreated as if something had forced him back toward the chair beside Miriam. He sat down, saying:

"No. It's impossible. It's incredible."

Said asked quietly:

"You're in the army? Who are you fighting? Why?"

The young man jumped to his feet.

"You have no right to ask those questions. You're on the other side."

"I? I'm on the other side?"

Said laughed heartily. And with that explosive laughter he felt as if he were pushing out all the pain and tension and fear and anguish in his chest. He wanted to keep on laughing and laughing until the entire world was turned upside down or until he fell asleep or died or raced out to his car. But the young man cut him off sharply.

"I see no reason to laugh."

"I do."

He laughed a little longer then stopped and became silent as suddenly as he had burst out laughing. He leaned back in his chair, feeling his calmness return, fishing through his pockets for a cigarette.

The silence lengthened. Then Safiyya, who had composed herself, asked in a subdued voice:

"Don't you feel that we are your parents?"

No one knew to whom the question was addressed. Miriam certainly didn't understand it, nor did the tall young man. As for Said, he didn't answer. He finished his cigarette then went over to the table to put it out. He felt a compulsion in the

process to rip the cap from its place, so he did, smiling scornful-
ly, then went back and sat down.

At that, the young man, his voice completely changed, said:

"We need to talk like civilized people."

Again, Said laughed.

"You don't want to negotiate, isn't that right? You said you
and I are on opposite sides. What happened? Do you want to
negotiate, or what?"

Agitated, Safiyya asked:

"What did he say?"

"Nothing."

The youth stood up again. He began to speak as though he
had prepared the sentences long ago.

"I didn't know that Miriam and Iphrat weren't my parents
until about three or four years ago. From the time I was small I
was a Jew . . . I went to Jewish school, I studied Hebrew, I go to
Temple, I eat kosher food . . . When they told me I wasn't their
own child, it didn't change anything. Even when they told me—
later on—that my original parents were Arabs, it didn't change
anything. No, nothing changed, that's certain. After all, in the
final analysis, man is a cause."[34]

"Who said that?"

"Said what?"

"Who said that man is a cause?"

"I don't know. I don't remember. Why do you ask?"

"Curiosity. Actually, just because that's exactly what was
going through my mind at this moment."

"That man is a cause?"

"Exactly."

"Then why did you come looking for me?"

"I don't know. Maybe because I didn't know it, or to be
more certain about it. I don't know. Anyway, go on."

The young man began pacing again with his hands clasped
behind his back: three steps toward the door, three steps toward
the table. He seemed to be trying to recall a long lesson learned
by heart. Cut off in the middle, he didn't know how to finish, so
he reviewed the first part silently in his head in order to be able
to continue. Abruptly, he said:

"After I learned that you were Arabs, I kept asking myself:

How could a father and mother leave their five-month-old son behind and run off? How could a mother and father not his own raise him and educate him for twenty years? Twenty years? Do you wish to say anything, sir?"

"No," Said replied briefly and decisively, motioning with his hand for him to continue.

"I'm in the Reserves now. I haven't been in direct combat yet so I can't describe my feelings . . . but perhaps in the future I'll be able to confirm to you what I'm about to say now: I belong here, and this woman is my mother. I don't know the two of you, and I don't feel anything special toward you."

"There's no need for you to describe your feelings to me later on. Maybe your first battle will be with a *fida'i*[35] named Khalid. Khalid is my son. I beg you to notice that I did not say he's your brother. As you said, man is a cause. Last week Khalid joined the *fidayeen*. Do you know why we named him Khalid and not Khaldun? Because we always thought we'd find you, even if it took twenty years. But it didn't happen. We didn't find you, and I don't believe we will find you."

Said rose heavily. Only now did he feel tired, that he had lived his life in vain. These feelings gave way to an unexpected sorrow, and he felt himself on the verge of tears. He knew it was a lie, that Khalid hadn't joined the *fidayeen*. In fact, he himself was the one who had forbidden it. He'd even gone so far as to threaten to disown Khalid if he defied him and joined the resistance. The few days that had passed since then seemed to him a nightmare that ended in terror. Was it really he who, just a few days ago, threatened to disown his son Khalid? What a strange world! And now, he could find no way to defend himself in the face of this tall young man's disavowal other than boasting of his fatherhood of Khalid—the Khalid whom he prevented from joining the *fidayeen* by means of that worthless whip he used to call fatherhood! Who knows? Perhaps Khalid had taken advantage of his being here in Haifa to flee. If only he had! What a failure his presence here would turn out to be if he returned and found Khalid waiting at home.

He moved a few steps forward and once again began to count the peacock feathers in the wooden vase. For the first time since the young man came into the room, Said looked at Miriam, and said to her slowly:

"He asks how a father and mother could leave their infant child and run off. Madame, you did not tell him the truth. And when you did tell him, it was too late. Are we the ones who left him? Are we the ones who killed that child near Bethlehem Church in Hadar? The child whose body, so you said, was the first thing that shocked you in this world that wipes out justice with baseness every day? Maybe that child was Khaldun! Maybe the small thing that died that wretched day was Khaldun. Yes, it was Khaldun. You lied to us. It was Khaldun. He died. This young man is none other than an orphan child you found in Poland or England."

The young man had withdrawn into himself in the chair, defeated. Said thought: "We've lost him, but surely he's lost himself after all this. He'll never be the same as he was an hour ago." This gave him some deep, inexplicable satisfaction and propelled him toward the chair where the young man sat. He stood in front of him and said:

"Man, in the final analysis, is a cause. That's what you said. And it's true. But what cause? That's the question! Think carefully. Khalid is also a cause, not because he's my son. In fact . . . but put the details, in any case, aside. When we talk about man, it has nothing to do with flesh and blood and identity cards and passports. Can you understand that? Good. Let's imagine that you received us—as we've dreamed for twenty years—with embraces and kisses and tears. Would that have changed anything? Even if you had accepted us, would we accept you? Let your name be Khaldun or Dov or Ishmael or anything else . . . what changes? In spite of it all, I don't feel any scorn toward you. The guilt isn't yours alone. Maybe the guilt will become your fate from this moment on. But beyond that, what? Isn't a human being made up of what's injected into him hour after hour, day after day, year after year? If I regret anything, it's that I believed the opposite for twenty years!"

He resumed his pacing, trying to appear as calm as possible, then returned to his seat. In the few steps it took to pass by the inlaid table where the peacock feathers swayed in the wooden

vase, everything seemed completely changed from when he had
first entered the room a few hours before. Then, he asked himself: What is a homeland? He smiled bitterly and allowed himself to drop, as one lets an object drop, into his chair. Safiyya
was looking at him with alarm. Her eyes grew wider, questioning, and it occurred to Said that he might draw her into the
matter.

"What is a homeland?"

She leaned forward, surprised, as though she didn't believe
what she heard. She asked with a delicacy that contained uncertainty:

"What did you say?"

"I said, what is a homeland? I was asking myself that question a moment ago. Naturally. What is a homeland? Is it these
two chairs that remained in this room for twenty years? The
table? Peacock feathers? The picture of Jerusalem on the wall?
The copper lock? The oak tree? The balcony? What is a homeland? Khaldun? Our illusions about him? Fathers? Their sons?
What is a homeland? With respect to Faris al-Lubda, what is a
homeland? Is it the picture of his brother hanging on the wall?
I'm only asking."

Once again, Safiyya began to weep. She dried her tears with
a small white handkerchief. Looking at her, Said thought: "How
this woman has aged. She squandered her youth waiting for this
moment, not knowing what a terrible moment it would be."

He looked at Dov again and it seemed to him utterly
impossible that he could have been born of this woman. He
tried to make out some similarity between Dov and Khalid, but
he couldn't find any resemblance between them. Instead, he saw
a difference between the two that verged on making them total
opposites. It amazed him that he'd lost any affection toward
Dov. He imagined that all his memories of Khaldun were a
handful of snow that the blazing sun had suddenly shone upon
and melted.

He was still looking at him when Dov got up and stood
stiffly in front of Said as if at the head of some hidden army
battalion. He was making an effort to be calm.

"Perhaps none of that would have happened if you'd
behaved the way a civilized and careful man should behave."

"What?"

"You[36] should not have left Haifa. If that wasn't possible, then no matter what it took, you should not have left an infant in its crib. And if that was also impossible, then you should never have stopped trying to return. You say that too was impossible? Twenty years have passed, sir! Twenty years! What did you do during that time to reclaim your son? If I were you I would've borne arms for that. Is there any stronger motive? You're all weak! Weak! You're bound by heavy chains of backwardness and paralysis! Don't tell me you spent twenty years crying! Tears won't bring back the missing or the lost. Tears won't work miracles! All the tears in the world won't carry a small boat holding two parents searching for their lost child. So you spent twenty years crying. That's what you tell me now? Is this your dull, worn-out weapon?"

Said drew back, shocked and stricken, overcome by vertigo. Could all this be true? Or was it just a long, drawn-out dream, an oppressive nightmare covering him like a horrible octopus? He looked at Safiyya, whose shock had taken the form of helpless collapse. He felt a deep sadness for her sake. Just to avoid appearing foolish he went over to her and said shakily:

"I don't want to argue with him."

"What did he say?"

"Nothing. Well, he said we're cowards."

Safiyya asked innocently:

"And because we're cowards, he can become like this?"

With that Said turned to the youth, who was still standing rigidly. The peacock feathers behind him seemed to form the tail of a large khaki-colored bird, the sight of which animated Said unexpectedly.

"My wife asks if the fact that we're cowards gives you the right to be this way. As you can see, she innocently recognizes that we were cowards. From that standpoint you are correct. But that doesn't justify anything for you. Two wrongs do not make a right. If that were the case, then what happened to Iphrat and Miriam in Auschwitz was right. When are you[37] going to stop considering that the weakness and the mistakes of others are endorsed over to the account of your own prerogatives? These old catchwords are worn out, these mathematical equations are full of cheating. First you say that our mistakes justify your mistakes, then you say that one wrong doesn't absolve another. You use the first logic to justify your presence here, and the second to avoid the punishment your presence here deserves. It seems to me you greatly enjoy this strange game. Here again, you're trying to fashion a race horse out of our weakness and mount its back. No, I'm not decreeing that you're an Arab. Now I know, better than anyone, that man is a cause, not flesh and blood passed down from generation to generation like a merchant and his client exchanging a can of chopped meat. I'm decreeing that in the final analysis you're a human being, Jewish or whatever you want. You must come to understand things as they should be understood. I know that one day you'll realize these things, and that you'll realize that the greatest crime any human being can commit, whoever he may be, is to believe even for one moment that the weakness and mistakes of others give him the right to exist at their expense and justify his own mistakes and crimes."

He was quiet for a moment, then looked directly into Dov's eyes.

"And you, do you believe we'll continue making mistakes? If we should stop making mistakes one day, what would be left for you then?"

He had a feeling that they should get up and leave, for everything had come to an end, and there was nothing more to say. At that moment he felt a deep longing for Khalid and wished he could fly to him and embrace him and kiss him and cry on his shoulder, reversing the roles of father and son in some unique, inexplicable way. "This is the homeland." He said it to himself, smiling, then turned to his wife:

"Do you know what the homeland is, Safiyya? The homeland is where none of this can happen."

"What happened to you, Said?"

"Nothing. Nothing at all. I was just asking. I'm looking for the true Palestine, the Palestine that's more than memories, more than peacock feathers, more than a son, more than scars written by bullets on the stairs. I was just saying to myself: What's Palestine with respect to Khalid? He doesn't know the vase or the picture or the stairs or Halisa or Khaldun. And yet for him, Palestine is something worthy of a man bearing arms for, dying for. For us, for you and me, it's only a search for something buried beneath the dust of memories. And look what we found beneath that dust. Yet more dust. We were mistaken when we thought the homeland was only the past. For Khalid, the homeland is the future. That's how we differed and that's why Khalid wants to carry arms. Tens of thousands like Khalid won't be stopped by the tears of men searching in the depths of their defeat for scraps of armor and broken flowers. Men like Khalid are looking toward the future, so they can put right our mistakes and the mistakes of the whole world. Dov is our shame, but Khalid is our enduring honor. Didn't I tell you from the beginning that we shouldn't come—because that was something requiring a war? Let's go!"

Khalid knew it before we did . . . Oh Safiyya! . . . Oh![38]

He stood up and Safiyya stood beside him, twisting her handkerchief in confusion. Dov remained seated, withdrawn. His cap was resting against the vase again, and it seemed, for some reason, ridiculous. Miriam said slowly:
"You can't leave like this. We haven't talked about it enough."
Said replied:
"There's absolutely nothing more to say. For you, perhaps the whole thing was just bad luck. But history isn't like that. When we came here we were resisting it, like we were, I admit, when we left Haifa. However, all of that is only temporary. Do you know something, madame? It seems to me every Palestinian is going to pay a price. I know many who have paid with their sons. I know now that I, too, paid with a son, in a strange way, but I paid him as a price . . . That was my first installment, and it's something that will be hard to explain."
He turned. Dov was still withdrawn in his chair, holding his head between his hands. When Said reached the door, he said:
"You two may remain in our house temporarily. It will take a war to settle that."
He started down the stairs, looking at everything carefully. It all seemed less important than it had a few hours earlier,

incapable of arousing any deep feeling in him. He heard the sound of Safiyya's footsteps behind him, more confident than before. The road outside was nearly empty. He headed for the car and let it coast noiselessly to the foot of the slope. Only at the bend did he start the engine and head for King Faisal Street.

They were silent all the way. They didn't utter a word until they reached the edge of Ramallah. Only then did he look at his wife and say:

"I pray that Khalid will have gone—while we were away!"

—translated by Karen E. Riley

Notes to *Returning to Haifa*

Returning to Haifa was published in 1969 under the title, *'A'id ila Hayfa.* Since its brevity suggests a novella, it is referred to as such here. However, it is generally referred to in Arabic as a novel to distinguish it from the great number of Kanafani's works that were short stories.

I have translated the original Arabic as literally as possible for reasons more fully set forth in the Introduction. But certain devices such as the use of contractions, particularly in the dialogue, were chosen not so much because Kanafani uses the colloquial as his writing tool (as Tawfiq al-Hakim does, for example, in his plays), but because he expresses the feelings and experiences of his characters with an intimacy and immediacy that warrants the use of such language in English. In the interest of appealing to the nonscholarly reader, I have also used common spellings for Arabic words and proper names if they are well known in English, and simple transliterations for those not commonly known. Idioms or specific vocabulary with no English equivalents are noted and explained where necessary. Annotations to the text have also been included in order to "level the playing field" for the general reader, clarifying references to places, people, or events that would be instantly familiar to the Palestinian reader (or most any Arabic-speaking reader in 1969) from personal experience or oral tradition.

—K. E. R.

1. In the June 1967 war, in addition to taking East Jerusalem, Israeli forces captured the Sinai Peninsula, the West Bank, the Gaza Strip, and the Golan Heights. The offensive against Syria began on

June 9, after Egypt and Jordan were defeated, so the entire Israeli force was concentrated directly on Syria. In twenty-seven hours Israel swept through the Golan Heights and was on the verge of reaching Damascus when a ceasefire was signed on June 11. The Mandelbaum Gate was the main passage between West Jerusalem, belonging to Israel, and East Jerusalem, controlled by Jordan between 1948–1967. The gate was torn down by Israel, "reuniting" Jerusalem after the June 1967 war.

2. In the aftermath of the 1948 war, Jordan annexed the West Bank, and Palestinians living there were officially subject to Jordanian rule, hence the Jordanian plates on Said S.'s car shortly after the 1967 war. Most Arabic geographical names were replaced with Hebrew in the part of Palestine that became Israel.

3. Literally, *Why? For the blackness of your eyes and my eyes?*

4. The city of Haifa is built on three levels determined by elevations that stretch back from the Mediterranean coast toward and up Mount Carmel. In 1948, the first and second levels had developed sufficiently to be contiguous, but the highest level was sparsely populated and separated from the lower two levels by a wide band of undeveloped property. *Halisa* was one of the Arab residential quarters of Haifa that were located on the first level adjoining the port; the Old City and the business district were also located on the first level. *Hadar Ha-Carmel* was the main Jewish residential neighborhood and administrative center of Haifa, located on the second level; it remains so today as well as being Haifa's commercial center. The highest level, *Har Ha-Carmel,* is residential and also contains recreational areas. *Wadi* means the course of a dry river or stream bed through which water may flow in wet seasons or after flash floods. *Wadi Nisnas* is the name of a residential quarter as well as of a wadi on the northwest edge of the business district.

5. *Wadi Rushmiyya:* A wadi on the southeast edge of the business district. A strategically important bridge spanned Wadi Rushmiyya over which all eastbound traffic out of Haifa flowed. A concrete structure that served as the control tower for bridge traffic was the site of a fierce confrontation between Arab and Jewish soldiers at the beginning of the battle for Haifa. After the founding of Israel, the bridge and wadi were renamed *Gibborim* ("Heroes") and a plaque was placed on the control tower commemorating the Jewish soldiers who died in battle there. *Burj,* meaning "tower," was the name of a street in Haifa and also a Turkish fortification dating from the late eighteenth or early nineteenth century.

6. Compare this scene with the following eyewitness accounts:

A rumor swept through town that the British army stood
ready to transfer out of Haifa anyone who was able to
reach the port. 'A panic-stricken stampede began heading
towards the gates of the port. Men trampled on their
brothers, women on their children. The boats in the harbor quickly filled with human cargo.' *The Palestine War
1947–1948: The Official Israeli Version* [Hebrew, tr. to
Arabic by Ahmad Khalifa] (Beirut: Mu'assasat al-Dirasat
al-Filastiniyya, 1984), 469.

The majority of the population panicked and thousands
surged out of the town into the port whence they were
evacuated to Acre. While they were thus in full flight they
were engaged by the advanced Jewish posts which inflict-
ed a number of casualties on them. R. D. Wilson, "The
Battle for Haifa," in Rashid Khalidi, ed., *From Haven to
Conquest* (Washington: The Institute for Palestine Studies,
1987), 773.

They could only flee in one direction: as the Zionist
Jerusalem Post openly reported the next day about the
exodus, it was an offensive 'forcing them to flee by the
only open escape route—the sea.' The flight to the harbor
down the narrow lanes, with children and older people
being trampled to death and drowning in overloaded
boats, was accompanied by clearly directed Zionist firing
on them. *The Jerusalem Post,* April 23, 1948; and R. D.
Wilson, *Cordon and Search: With the 6th Airborne Division
in Palestine* (Aldershot, England: Gale & Polden, 1949),
193; both cited in Erskine B. Childers, "The Wordless
Wish: From Citizens to Refugees," in Ibrahim Abu-
Lughod, ed., *The Transformation of Palestine* (Evanston,
Illinois: Northwestern University Press, 1971), 189–190.

7. *Bat Gallim:* Hebrew, meaning "daughter of the waves." It is
written incorrectly in the Arabic as *Bayt* (Arabic for "house") *Gallim.*
Bat Gallim is the northwestern tip of Haifa; it protrudes into the sea,
forming a beach. The road into Haifa from the south follows the
Mediterranean coast straight north, circles the Bat Gallim promonto-

ry, then heads east and south into Haifa proper, where the city borders Haifa Bay. Hence, Bat Gallim is the first part of Haifa reached by a traveler approaching from the south.

8. The names are all derived from the same three-letter Arabic root, *kh-l-d,* meaning "to remain" or "last forever." *Khaldun* is a true proper name derived from the root, meaning "those who are immortal." *Khalid* (fem. *Khalida*) is an adjective of general usage as well as a proper name and means "eternal," "enduring." The use of the same root for the children born later signifies a desire to keep alive the memory of the firstborn without directly admitting his possible death by assigning his exact name to another child. *Abu* means "father of." Traditionally, an Arab father is known as "father of" his firstborn son. Said S. thus would have been known as Abu Khaldun had he wished to acknowledge the existence of the child left behind.

9. *Galilee* and *Muthallath:* Galilee comprises the northern area between the Mediterranean and the Jordan River/Sea of Galilee; Muthallath extends into the Kingdom of Jordan. *Safad* is a town in Galilee.

10. *Masatib,* plural of *mastaba:* A *mastaba* is a stone bench built into the side of a house, or a bench-height stone wall surrounding a house, enclosing a patio area outside of the house. The reference to iron grillwork of the *masatib* seems incongruous; however, a photograph of the Kanafani family's own house in Acre shows a stone wall surrounding the house with an iron grillwork fence extending upward out of the stone. The stone and iron appear to form a flush surface from the outside, but the photograph is accompanied by a reference to someone "sitting" on the *mastaba.* This would lead one to believe that the stone portion extended out beyond the iron grillwork on the inside, indeed forming a "bench" facing the inside of the enclosed area. Perhaps this is what is referred to here in the novel.

11. *Umm* means "mother of" (see Note 8). Kanafani's use of *Umm Khalid* to identify Safiyya here emphasizes Safiyya's changed relationship to the house since she last saw it.

12. *Haganah* (Hebrew, meaning "defense"): Military organization tracing its roots back to early Jewish settlers living in Palestine under Ottoman rule, who banded together for protection calling themselves *Shomrim* ("watchmen"), and later *Hashomer* ("the watchman"). With the establishment of the British Mandate in 1922, the Hashomer was disbanded and reorganized on a national level by Jewish labor groups and renamed *Haganah.* The Haganah eventually came under the direction of the Jewish Agency and upon passage of the United

Nations partition plan was merged with other military groups and named *Tzva Haganah Leyisrael* ("Israeli Defense Force"), the name by which the Israeli army is still known today.

13. The Bureau of Absentee Property was a division of the Jewish Agency established to administer property formerly belonging to Arab Palestinians who fled Palestine in 1947–1948.

14. The Jewish Agency was established by the Mandate to aid in "such economic, social and other matters as may affect the establishment of the Jewish national home and the interests of the Jewish population in Palestine." An infrastructure of social, political, labor, and military institutions grew out of the Jewish Agency for the benefit of the Jewish population in Palestine. "The Mandate for Palestine, 24 July 1922," in Fred J. Khouri, *The Arab-Israeli Dilemma,* 3rd ed. (Syracuse: Syracuse University Press, 1985), 527–528.

15. Arthur Koestler, *Thieves in the Night* (New York: The Macmillan Company, 1946). The novel presents a highly romanticized account of a group of idealistic young Jews who escape Nazi persecution and establish a settlement in Palestine in the late 1930s. It projects an image of a land of isolated beauty and tranquility, peopled by a few strong pioneering souls struggling to forge a new future in the face of all manner of hostility and adversity. A few excerpts:

> About half-past five a slight inflammation over the hills to the east showed that the sky was preparing for the rise of day . . . . The new settlers found themselves in the centre of a landscape of gentle desolation, a barrenness mellowed by age. The rocks had settled down for eternity; the sparse scrubs and olive trees exhaled a silent and contented resignation. (pp. 29–30)

> But the distant hills were merely the frame of the picture; the feast for Joseph's eyes was the green Valley of Jezreel itself, the cradle of the Communes. Twenty years ago a desolate marsh cursed with all the Egyptian plagues, it had now become a continuous chain of settlements which stretched like a string of green pearls across the country's neck from Haifa to the Jordan. (p. 228)

> Far off in the night a light had begun to blink; it looked like a red spark suspended in the air . . . .
> The distant spark went rhythmically on and off, flash

and darkness, flash, flash and darkness, flash and flash, dot
and dash . . . .

They are sending Isaiah in Morse:
And they shall build houses and inhabit them; and they
shall plant vineyards, and eat the fruit of them. (p. 357)

16. Refers to the often quoted slogan, "a land without people for
a people without land," coined by early Zionist writers around the
turn of this century and eventually adopted by the Zionist movement
as a whole to press its claims for the biblical land of Israel promised by
God to the Jewish people. The Jews were driven out from Palestine by
the Romans in the first century A.D., and in certain religious and
Zionist political writings, the land was described as having lain empty,
unpeopled, and uncultivated during the intervening two thousand
years.

17. Moshe Zalitsky Carmel, Commander of the Carmeli Brigade
centered in Haifa, one of the nine *Palmach* battalions in Palestine. The
Palmach ("Shock Force") were commando units of the Haganah set
up in the 1940s.

18. Describes "Operation *Misparayim.*" Britain had announced
withdrawal from Haifa for the end of April; then on April 20, she
abruptly informed both Jewish and Arab leaders in Haifa that withdrawal would occur that very day. The Zionist forces immediately
went into action. A three-pronged attack, called Operation
Misparayim ("scissors"), was launched on the city and lasted two days.
The plan consisted of sending one battalion to occupy the Arab district, another to descend from Mount Carmel toward the commercial
center, and a third to go up out of the business district, which was also
under Jewish control, to meet the Carmel battalion and cut the city in
two. *The Palestine War,* 468.

19. *Irgun:* Also known as *Irgun Tzvai Leumi* ("National Military
Organization"), or *ETZEL.* Founded in 1937 and led by Menachem
Begin, it broke with the "defensive" Haganah and advocated "offen-
sive" action in seeking to end the British Mandate and establish a
Jewish state. Later, a yet more radical splinter group broke from the
Irgun and was called the *Lohamie Herut Yisrael* ("Fighters for Israel's
Freedom") or *LEHI,* and was known as the "Stern Gang" after its
founder, Avraham Yair Stern.

20. Major General Hugh Stockwell, British Commander of
Northern Palestine, with responsibility for the British forces in Haifa
during the windup of the mandate.

21. Whether or not both Arab and Jewish leaders were informed simultaneously of the imminent British withdrawal has been disputed. Official Israeli government documents state that both were informed at the same time and that the Jews were the first to take advantage of the void left by the British withdrawal by launching their three-pronged attack. The same source also credits the Jews with having superior arms and strategic location in Haifa at the time. *The Palestine War,* 467. British army officer Major R. D. Wilson also states that both sides were informed within an hour of each other, but the assertion is refuted by Walid Khalidi in a footnote, stating that the Jews were given enough advance notice to prepare their attack. *From Haven to Conquest,* 771–773.

22. Saturday is the Jewish Sabbath, during which certain Jewish denominations proscribe the driving of automobiles. Friday is the Muslim Sabbath and Sunday, the Christian. Historically, peoples of all three religions have lived in Palestine, and Jerusalem contains sites held sacred by all three.

23. Through some error, the original date reads "the 30th of April."

24. Acre is a port city north of Haifa located on a promontory and built around a crescent-shaped bay, the main part of the city lying on its western shore. Acre was originally included in the territory allotted to the Arab state by the United Nations partition plan, hence Palestinians evacuated from Haifa were taken to Acre, a boat ride of approximately one hour away. During the mandate, the British maintained their central prison for Palestine in a fortification in Acre, this prison being the site of executions by the British of Zionists convicted of capital crimes under mandatory law.

25. *Ibn:* Means "son of." A man may be known as "son of" his father, particularly if his father is a prominent person. Safiyya here is clarifying that she is thinking of the same person Said refers to when he mentions their former neighbor by his given name, *Faris* al-Lubda, rather than as *Ibn* al-Lubda, the name by which Safiyya apparently knows him.

26. Convent and School of the *Freres des Ecoles Chretiennes,* French missionary schools located in several cities in Palestine.

27. *Manshiyya:* Arab residential quarter in Jaffa, the center of strong and well-organized resistance. The Irgun also had forces in the Manshiyya, and in the early months of 1948 armed conflicts took place between the two sides in the district. The British remained in Jaffa for about a week after their withdrawal from Haifa. Wanting to

avoid a repetition of the mass panic and exodus that had just taken place there, they sent reconnaissance planes over the Manshiyya to survey the Irgun positions and later bombed them. In the final days of April and the first of May 1948, fierce fighting took place among the three factions, with the result that the quarter was almost completely destroyed. What remained was eventually razed by the Israelis for urban development. See *The Palestine War,* 446–449.

28. *Tall al-Rish* (also known as *Tel al-Rish; tall* is Arabic, and *tel,* Hebrew, for "hill"): Originally an Arab town, later a Jewish settlement south of Jaffa.

29. This is the first instance of Kanafani's use of the plural. See Introduction, Note 6.

30. *Shatt al-Shabab:* Literally, "young mens' coast." No reference to its location was found.

31. Possibly a reference to the fact that the British at first bombed Irgun positions in Jaffa (Note 27) to try to keep Zionist forces from seizing the city, but in the end withdrew. May also refer to the armies of the neighboring Arab countries which failed in their attempts to retake the areas of Palestine conquered by the Zionists.

32. Kanafani uses the plural from here to the end of the paragraph.

33. Refers to the Sinai war of 1956 in which Israel invaded the Sinai Peninsula after Egyptian president Gamal Abdel Nasser nationalized the Suez Canal and closed it to Israeli and other foreign shipping.

34. The statement, *man is a cause* (*al-insan huwa qadiyya*) was taken by Muhammad Siddiq as the title of his book examining the development of political consciousness in Ghassan Kanafani's fiction. The statement itself is ambiguous, since the word *qadiyya* "can be rendered as 'cause,' 'problem,' or 'case,' among other possibilities." Siddiq notes that the "abstract quality of the last sentence" distinguishes it from the rest of Dov's discourse and says that the statement "plays a key role in the novel." In applying the statement to the characters and implications of the novel, Siddiq states that Said's and Safiyya's shortcomings are mitigated by the "moral injustice" they have suffered, while Miriam's "commendable character traits and Dov's correct logic appear less compelling when appended to an unjust cause." Muhammad Siddiq, *Man is a Cause* (Seattle: University of Washington Press, 1984), 57–62.

35. *Fida'i,* singular of *fidayeen:* A fighter willing to sacrifice his life for his cause. The term is applied especially to Palestinian free-

dom-fighters, guerillas, or commandos—whatever political faction
they belong to—who are ready to sacrifice their lives in armed struggle for the cause of regaining their homeland.

36. In this paragraph Kanafani uses the plural throughout except
in the seventh, eighth, and final three sentences where he uses the singular.

37. Again, Kanafani intersperses the plural pronoun starting here
and through the fourth sentence, denoting that Said, in response to
Dov's condemnation moments before, is now addressing the Jewish
community as a whole.

38. The setting off of Said's seemingly disconnected thoughts
appears to be deliberate in the original, suggesting Said's anguish as
well as his sense of resolve building from his new-found self-discov-
ery. It is an interesting example of Kanafani's ability to move easily
between realism and lyricism, melding the prosaic and the poetic.

Acknowledgments

WE BOTH WOULD LIKE TO EXPRESS OUR DEEP appreciation to Anni Kanafani and the Ghassan Kanafani Cultural Foundation for all their encouragement and for granting permission for these translations, as well as for graciously supplying corrections and personal recollections for the Biographical Essay. We would also like to thank Lynne Rienner for supporting our endeavor to make newly available this collection of Ghassan Kanafani's literary work.

—*B. H. and K. E. R.*

*   *   *

I would like to express my deep gratitude to Randa Shaath, who in reviewing these translations shared with me her knowledge of Palestine, its language and its traditions. I am grateful as well to Hasna Mekdashi, Ghanem Bibi, Farouq Ghandour, and Denys Johnson-Davies for their support and comments.

—*B. H.*

*   *   *

To Professor J. Moshief for conveying to me his sense of Arabic as a vital spoken language, to Deborah Meyers and Regina Hurwitz for their valuable guidance, and to Doris Safie for patiently editing the manuscript with skill and sensitivity, I would like to express my sincere appreciation. As always, I am grateful to my husband, Douglas Riva, for his unwavering support. To Palestinians everywhere, I express my gratitude for allowing me to learn from them the precious value of memory.

—*K. E. R.*

About the Book

"POLITICS AND THE NOVEL," GHASSAN KANAFANI once said, "are an indivisible case." Fadl al-Naqib has reflected that Kanafani "wrote the Palestinian story, then he was written by it." His narratives offer entry into the Palestinian experience of the conflict that has anguished the people of the Middle East for most of the twentieth century.

In *Palestine's Children*, each story involves a child—a child who is victimized by political events and circumstances, but who nevertheless participates in the struggle toward a better future. As in Kanafani's other fiction, these stories explore the need to recover the past—the lost homeland—by action. At the same time, written by a major talent, they have a universal appeal.

This entirely new edition includes the translators' contextual introduction and a short biography of the author.

Born in Acre (northern Palestine) in 1936, **Ghassan Kanafani** was a prominent spokesman for the Popular Front for the Liberation of Palestine and founding editor of its weekly magazine *Al-Hadaf*. His novels and short stories have been published in sixteen languages. He, along with his niece, was killed in Beirut in 1972 in the explosion of his booby-trapped car.